Gabi reach  **fluffy towels to wrap her**

As sh ... touch ... hers, ... Onc ... felt ... she' ... him. ... gaze ... to echo what she felt ... light touch against her fingers brought her the oddest sense of mutual attraction, of loneliness dispelled, of welcome, of coming ho—

She gasped when she realized where her thoughts were going. She couldn't go there. She just couldn't. This wasn't home, and this man was all wrong for her.

Wrong, wrong, wrong.

She had to get away. Now. No matter how many dogs she left behind. As she'd thought a number of times before, her sanity depended on it. No matter what she felt whenever she was in Zach's presence.

Books by Ginny Aiken

Love Inspired

The Daddy Surprise
A Daughter's Homecoming

Love Inspired Suspense

Mistaken for the Mob
Mixed up with the Mob
Married to the Mob
*Danger in a Small Town
*Suspicion
*Someone to Trust

*Carolina Justice

GINNY AIKEN

Born in Havana, Cuba, raised in Valencia and Cara-cas, Venezuela, Ginny Aiken discovered books early and wrote her first novel at age fifteen while she trained with the Ballets de Caracas, later known as the Venezuelan National Ballet. She burned that tome when she turned a "mature" sixteen. Stints as report-er, paralegal, choreographer, language teacher and retail salesperson followed. Her life as wife, mother of four boys and herder of their numerous and as-sorted friends brought her back to books and writing in search of her sanity. She's now the author of more than twenty published works and a frequent speaker at Christian women's and writers' workshops, but has yet to catch up with that elusive sanity.

A Daughter's Homecoming

Ginny Aiken

HARLEQUIN® LOVE INSPIRED®

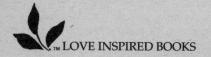 LOVE INSPIRED BOOKS

Recycling programs
for this product may
not exist in your area.

ISBN-13: 978-0-373-81749-8

A DAUGHTER'S HOMECOMING

www.Harlequin.com

Printed in U.S.A.

And [I] will be your Father unto you, and ye shall
be my sons and daughters, saith the Lord Almighty.
—*2 Corinthians* 6:18

This one is dedicated to the memory of my late mother, Olga, and to my dad, Juan. Their home is on the Puget Sound, in a small town very much like Lyndon Point. Miss you, Mom. Love you, Dad.

Chapter One

~❧~

Lyndon Point, Washington State

With a heartfelt sigh, Gabriella Carlini stood up from where she'd sat for a moment's break. The top step of the back stoop to her parents' restaurant wasn't the finest place to rest, but it had been the best at that moment. She opened the kitchen door to Tony's and wrinkled her nose when the unpleasant tang struck her nostrils. She'd expected to find all kinds of disorganization when she got to Tony's, since her mother was at home caring for Gabi's ailing father instead of running the restaurant. But the actual state in which she'd found the place went far beyond a mess.

Food had spoiled when the teen part-timers her parents employed had refrigerated new deliveries and merely pushed the older supplies behind the new. Now she had bins of potatoes and onions gone bad, loaves of cheese and logs of pizza meats gone well beyond their sell-by dates and straight to spoiled, and the vegetable crispers were full of limp and unusable produce.

She should have come home when her mother called to tell her about her father's stroke, as she'd wanted to do. But Mama, as she still called her mother, in the old Italian way, had insisted Papa was receiving the best of care and she had everything under control....

How wrong she'd been!

Now, though, there was nothing to do but get back to work—as she'd been doing since nigh unto the crack of dawn. As she stepped inside, a flash of movement to her right in the alley out back caught her eye. When she turned to see what might have darted past the Dumpster, nothing struck her as out of the ordinary in the grubby concrete landscape. The thought of a rat turned her already iffy stomach. She scooted inside and slammed the steel door shut, then went straight to the massive metal refrigerator to throw out more of the old food.

With her hand outstretched to the refrigerator door's latch handle, she sent a prayer heavenward. "Lord, please don't let rats have taken up residence in the alley. I still have a number of trips' worth of trash to haul out before I can seek sanctuary in the kitchen. I'll clean out foul refrigerators any day, gladly wash sticky shelves, scrub grungy floors, but—ugh!" She shuddered at the thought of an encounter of the rodent kind.

"Hey, Miss Carlini."

She jumped inches off the ground. "Dylan!" Her heart pounded like a bass drum. "You shouldn't sneak up on anyone like that, you know?"

"Sorry, ma'am." The lanky nineteen-year-old with a painful-looking stud through his eyebrow and a map of crooked roadways carved through his quarter-inch-long buzz-cut hair came close. Then he waved toward the kitchen. "I'm so sorry about what happened earlier. I never knew how soon all that food would go bad, plus when the delivery truck brought new cheese and sausage and stuff...well, I guess Kirstie and I didn't think about using the old stuff up first. If there's anything I can do..."

Feeling about a thousand years old every time he called her Miss Carlini—or worse, ma'am—Gabi let the fridge door close. Dylan had already apologized five times that morning. "Tell you what. First, call me Gabi. Then you have to remember that sauce spoils in five days, even in a fridge. And then you can make it up to me by emptying the last bin under the counter. We'll figure out the next step in our plan of attack after that."

Dylan darted his gaze toward the dining room, the bin and her. Gabi wondered if he might be weighing the merits of bailing on his part-time job.

But then he squared his shoulders and gave a tight nod. "I'll go get a trash bag."

Thank You, Lord! Although she wished she didn't need to recruit the teen for the unpleasant task, she had little chance of getting the job done quickly without his help. They had to clean it all up before health department authorities showed up for a random check of the premises, which they were known to do. That could spell disaster. For Tony's…and for her family.

As she opened the refrigerator, she heard a sound behind her, near the kitchen door. She paused, listened.

Nothing.

"Strange." She must have imagined it.

After taking—and holding—a deep breath, Gabi opened the crisper drawer.

The faint noise rang out again.

Then yet again.

Ears alert to any further sound, she glanced toward the dining room. Three teenage part-timers were setting up for lunch, so she was on her own in the kitchen. Obviously *something* had made that noise…but what? Shoulders squared, she closed the refrigerator, then headed toward the back, pausing when she reached the door, praying for protection from rats. The rapid-fire metallic tap-tap-tap, scratch-scratch-scratch started up again.

Braced for whatever she might find, she very slowly pressed the door handle, then yanked.

"Oh, my…"

The sight on the other side stunned her. She never could have envisioned the little dog, part Jack Russell terrier, part unidentified shaggy, with long floppy ears, luminous brown eyes and, as a finishing touch, a thin C-shaped tail, which it immediately tucked between its legs. It shivered.

Even on this hot June morning.

As Gabi stared down at the filthy, bedraggled mutt, unsure of what to do next, the poor animal shook harder.

She took a step forward.

It dropped, then rolled onto its back, four paws in the air, still quaking without pause. That's when she realized how undernourished he was. Every rib tented saggy skin that showed blotches here and there, where patches of fur had either fallen or been yanked out. She didn't want to think along the latter lines, to imagine what kind of altercation might have caused the bare spots.

"Easy, boy," she crooned. "I won't let anyone hurt you. Let me come closer, now, to see what's up with those sores. I only want to help."

She dropped to her knees, aware that even her five-foot-two height would intimidate the little guy. Scooting closer, inch by inch, she continued cooing softly to keep him calm. After a couple of minutes, once she'd reached him, she noted how even more of the angry red blotches mapped his belly and scrawny chest. A blood-encrusted scrape on his right rear thigh looked like it might be the result of another animal's bite.

After a silent prayer, she extended a hand, not touching the dog, waiting to see if he would accept her. He froze. The shivers stopped. His brown eyes stared at her with laser focus. As she lowered her fingers to just a whisper away, he reached out and licked her palm.

"Hello there," she murmured. He licked again. And again.

Then he flipped up onto his four paws and went for her face, apparently intent on returning her show of kindness with a multitude of kisses. She backed up just out of his tongue's reach, not knowing the state of his health. She did, however, rub him under the side of his chin. He melted again at her touch.

From this close vantage point, he looked worse than before. He was half-starved, filthy, his coat matted beyond rescue by a good groomer, and all the skin she now saw between clumps of scruffy hair appeared red and irritated. She had to do something for the little guy.

"But I can't take you home with me," she said, more for her benefit than his. She sat at his side, taking a momentary break in the rubbing caresses.

"Mama has enough on her hands with Papa's recovery, and I'm going back to Cleveland as soon as possible. My landlord made a huge deal on the lease about pets—none allowed."

The dog nudged her hand with his moist black button nose. From deep in his throat came a string of growly conversational sounds, at the end of which he cocked his head to one side and stared.

When she didn't respond as he seemed to want, he let out a whiny whimper. His killer stare never let up.

"What am I going to do with you?"

He again nudged her hand, then began to lick fingers she figured stank of the garbage she'd dumped. "You're beyond hungry, aren't you? And...you know what? I can do much better than smelly fumes on my hands."

She settled him back on the floor and headed for the refrigerator. She rummaged inside, grabbed one of the five-pound chubs of hamburger she'd kept front and center after she'd disposed of the spoiled stuff, and verified the expiration date on the plastic wrapping.

"Perfect." She glanced at her new buddy. "You're going to love a chunk of this. Trust me."

In a few minutes, the scent of browning wholesome meat filled the kitchen. A clean, stainless-steel mixing bowl would do well as the pup's new dish. He piped up, letting out a handful of excited yips as he bounced in the air like a dirty, four-legged bouncy ball.

Gabi marveled at his spirited display. How could a creature as forsaken as this one muster so much energy? He was little more than stretched skin and sharp bone. As she smiled, the word *indomitable* came to mind.

When the meat had cooked through, she served up the dog's savory meal, stirred it to cool enough to make it safe for consumption and then set it down on the back stoop. After all, health ordinances did forbid animals in commercial kitchens.

She had to decide what to do with the half-starved stray. The half-starved stray who at that moment was eating hamburger as fast as he could, letting out appreciative grunts as he wolfed it all down.

She sat next to him to think through her dilemma.

"Hey, Miss…er…Gabi— Whoa!" Dylan caught the door he'd flung open to keep it from slamming into Gabi. And the dog.

The dog surprised her when he quit licking the now-empty bowl and scurried into her lap. He then growled a low, deep warning at the teen.

Dylan respected the threat with hands-to-shoulders in the universal sign of surrender. "All right. I got it. It's okay." Without looking away from the tiny canine, he spoke to Gabi. "Where'd he come from?"

"He scratched at the door. He's starving—literally."

The teen's look came full of doubt. "I don't think

feeding him's such a great idea. He might get the wrong impression." Dylan gave her a questioning look. "Or maybe…not so wrong?"

She shrugged.

He went on. "My mom's always said once you feed a stray, you're pretty much stuck with it for life."

"That better not be the case this time." She sighed. "I can't keep him."

"So what are you going to do with him?"

Her question precisely. "Not sure yet. I'm thinking."

"The animal shelter's got a new director." Dylan fingered the steel ball on the stud through his eyebrow. "He's supposed to have fixed it up, fired the slackers, hired new people, scrubbed even the ceiling and turned it into a no-kill place."

"And you know all this because…?"

He quirked his lips. "It was a real big deal in town a couple of months ago. The new director came up from Sacramento with all kinds of new ideas. Some people didn't like it, others loved it. But everybody had something to say about it."

"If you're sure it's a no-kill shelter, then it's probably the best place for this little guy."

"Unless you keep—"

"I know." She sighed again. She wished she could. Something about the ragtag critter drew her right in. Maybe it was his ready friendliness and overwhelming trust. Or maybe his eyes. "I can't. I really can't. I'm going back to my life in Cleveland as soon as things are settled here for my parents, and I can't keep pets in my rental."

"That's too bad." He gestured at the stray. "He really likes you."

The dog barked as though he agreed with Dylan. And with Gabi. The unexpectedly likable stray stared at her with his enormous brown eyes beneath that tangle of muddy brown hair. He tugged at her heart, but she couldn't change reality.

"Okay, then. That's the plan." She cradled the scrap of ratty fur and bones in her arms and then stood. "I'll take him over to the shelter. Can you hold down the fort while I'm gone? It won't take long."

After Dylan handed her the purse she kept on a shelf near the back door, Gabi hurried down the street to the old shelter building, stray in her arms. For years the place had been known as a dismal pit, populated with unwanted pets captured by Animal Control. It had been in need of a different kind of someone to take over the reins. She hoped this director knew what he was doing. The pooch in her arms and all the other discards deserved it.

Her little guy's pink tongue darted out and he licked her chin.

Tears welled in Gabi's eyes. He was going to make someone a great pal. Too bad it wouldn't be her.

* * *

For a thirty-year-old failure, Zachary Davenport figured he was finally getting it right. He turned off the water at the steel sink where they bathed the small and mid-size dogs relinquished to the Lyndon Point Animal Shelter and grabbed the towel on top of the tall stack of clean linen. A hint of the crisp, familiar scent of chlorine bleach in the fabric struck his senses, and he smiled in satisfaction.

When he'd first arrived to assume his position at the shelter, the only thing he'd smelled had been ammonia from unkempt animal cages. Shocked to the core, he'd fired every last employee and declared war against the sad conditions. He'd hired a new crew, invited a group of caring volunteers to join their efforts and bought all the commercial disinfectant cleaner he could get his hands on. Armed with scrub brushes and hoses, he and his team had set about to transform the shelter. His furry-haired charges might have been unwanted and mistreated in their previous situations, but now that they were under his care, they would have a much better quality of life.

He wiped up the water he'd splashed and dripped with his used towel before tossing it in the wheeled white-cloth laundry bin. As the managing director he didn't have to shoulder the minutiae of the rescue's daily chores, but he loved animals, and if he went too long without contact with the dogs and cats, he missed them.

He loved what he was doing these days.

What he didn't love were the occasional memories and jabs of guilt that struck when he least expected them. Zach wondered if he'd ever forget, if he would ever put his past behind him and really move on—

"Hey, boss!" Claudia called from the front desk, mercifully dragging him back to the present. "We've got a new one—just walked in—and he's cute, too. But I have to hit the road if I'm going to get to the orthodontist in time for Eva's appointment."

"Things are under control here, so go ahead." He hung up the waterproof apron and snagged an intake folder from his office on the way to the reception area. "Really, Claudia, there's nothing to worry about. As long as Oscar's still out back, he and I can handle whatever comes in while you're gone." He waved the folder as he pushed through the swinging door. "See? I'm prepared."

Claudia smiled, slung her bag over her shoulder and walked to the door. "See ya in a couple of hours!"

Another step, and Zach stopped. Oh, sure. The dog was cute. But the woman who held the filthy creature in her arms was much cuter. She stood, if lucky, a couple of inches over five feet, and her dirt-stained pink T-shirt and cutoff jean shorts displayed nicely rounded curves. On her feet, she wore a pair of pink flip-flops, revealing toenails painted hot pink.

She must really like the happy color.

She looked vaguely familiar, but he knew he'd never met her. He wouldn't have forgotten if he had.

A thin line etched itself between her eyebrows as midnight-dark eyes darted from the neat counter to the clean but worn chairs and finally to him. She nibbled her bottom lip. More than anything else, the riot of curls she wore leashed into a thick ponytail snared his gaze. The sunlight poured in through the glass front door and her inky-black locks caught it, reflecting back vibrancy and life. As he stared, he couldn't stop a smile.

He held out his hand in greeting, his gaze still on her swinging curls. "Hi. Zach Davenport, the shelter's director. How can I help you?"

She clamped her lips, then tipped up her rounded chin, arms tighter around the dog, who snuggled into the curve of her neck. Okay. The lady had rejected the handshake. The only thing on her mind was the filthiest Heinz 57 canine he'd seen in a long time. Feeling stupid, he slipped his hand back into his pants pocket and rattled the intake papers.

"Let's start with—"

"Please promise he'll get a fair deal here."

Zach blinked. Talk about direct. Fortunately, in this instance, he had a clear conscience. He smiled again and pointed to the No-Kill emblem on the glass door. "We don't give these fellows expiration dates, and we do our best for them. We clean them, feed them, nurse them to health if they need it, and do everything possible to find them good forever homes."

The stiffness in her shoulders eased a fraction as she clung to his every word.

The dog wriggled in her clutches.

She glanced down at her bundle of fur, and a slow, sweet grin revealed a dimple in her right cheek. But then she drew herself back up, squared her shoulders and met Zach's gaze.

Her brown eyes reminded him of melted chocolate, with their anxious expression. As his gaze latched on to hers, Zach felt a surprising need to reassure her about the dog's future care, so he took a step closer.

He caught himself, stopped. As appealing as she was, he was a *professional* and he couldn't afford to let this woman distract him from his work. She spoke again with the bedraggled pile of dirty dog held close as though it were Lassie or Benji or even Toto come back to life. He gave her stray another look. Not a chance. This one was scruffy and muddy. Time to get to work. They had a dog in need to deal with.

He stepped closer, ready to take hold of her charge, then took a deep breath—and reared back. *Oof!*

The dog and his escort had come in on a wave of a strong, offensive odor. Zach knew he and the stray would be revisiting the animal-bathing tub immediately. This newest intake was in dire need of shampoo and lots of water.

Her cheeks colored to a pretty rose. "I'm sorry. He's a mess, and I've been— Well, I was cleaning out some spoiled…stuff. For lack of a better word, we're both quite smelly."

For a moment, he wondered about the "spoiled stuff," but then focused on the matter before him. "I see," he said in a mild tone. He reached for the scrap of canine in her arms. "So then…about the dog?"

A worried look drew her eyebrows together and her arms tightened the smallest bit.

The pup yipped.

Her deep inhale quivered. "He's not mine. I found him in the service alley behind my parents' business. He needs a home." She visibly pulled herself together again and nailed Zach with that penetrating stare again. "A *good* home. I'm here to make sure he gets one. And after I leave today, I will come back. To check up on him. As often as it takes to make sure things finally go his way."

Waving the intake folder, he stepped to her side, smell or no smell. "Let's see what I can do for you— er…for him."

Chapter Two

Gabi didn't get a good look at the man in the shelter until he stood right next to her, a folder tucked under one arm, his intention clear as he reached for her stray. The first thing that drew her attention from the dog to the director, alerting her to his nearness, was his clean, fresh scent. The aftershave he'd used sometime earlier in the day still lingered and offered a spicy hint of woody crispness, a welcome change after she'd spent the past couple of hours smelling a decided…um…*lack* of freshness.

The shelter director really was attractive. While not an overly tall man, maybe even a hair less than six feet, he still was much bigger than Gabi's five foot two. The navy blue scrub top he wore lay smooth across a broad chest and wide shoulders, suggesting solid power. His face, not model-handsome, had an outdoorsy bronze glow and exuded strength and character with those rugged lines, a nose with a bump that suggested a long-ago break, and that wide, easy grin. Twin sunbursts of smile creases at his temples bracketed gray eyes, and a shock of streaky dark blond hair brushed his forehead. He didn't look anything like Gabi would have imagined a man who spent his days indoors caring for homeless animals would look. While she'd naively expected a stereotypical lab tech with dark-rimmed glasses, this man appeared as though he belonged on a ski slope, training for Olympic races, or maybe climbing Mount Rainier, tethered to the rock face by some skinny rope and a handful of flimsy aluminum gadgets. Clearly, the new director didn't spend all his time inside, bathing dogs and plowing through mountains of paperwork. She wondered what kind of sport appealed to an animal lover.

Or, rather, someone she hoped was an animal lover.

What kind of man would choose this kind of work? What had made him become a shelter director instead of…oh…maybe a Forest Service wildlife biologist? It surprised her to note how this man she'd just met piqued her curiosity.

As her imagination ran amok, his voice rumbled through her. It resonated with a richness that drew her, its calm cadence a welcome invitation to relax. He probably used that comforting approach, that same warm voice to soothe anxious animals.

Then she realized he was waiting. For her response.

Great. She was making a splendid impression, all spaced out like that.

"…don't you like him?"

"Sorry," she mumbled. "I…ah…got distracted. You were saying?"

His distinctive gray eyes narrowed a fraction. "I wanted to know why you won't keep the little guy."

Gabi glanced at the rascal in her arms, the tug on her heart stronger than ever. She rubbed a finger over his head, and he leaned into her touch. The tug grew more insistent. "I wish I could, but I'm only in town to take care of a family matter. My landlord back home has a no-pet, no-exception rule. If I take this guy back to Cleveland with me, we'll both be homeless."

He arched a brow. "Cleveland, huh? Pretty far away. And you have family here?"

A family everyone in Lyndon Point knew. Only too well.

The shelter director's question revealed how new he was to town. All the longtime residents knew her by sight, definitely by the picture her parents kept behind the cash register at Tony's.

"I grew up here," she said, "but I left for college in Ohio. Once I finished my degrees, I found a job I love in Cleveland…and so I stayed. But my family is still here."

"Do you come back frequently?"

A blush crept up Gabi's cheeks. "Um…well, not as often as my parents would like."

Again, his brow rose, but he said nothing. He just studied her, and Gabi felt twitchier by the second. She wished she'd taken the time to clean up. Looking—and smelling—like she must by now from cleaning that mess of a kitchen and hugging a stray dog, he had her at a huge disadvantage. Especially since he seemed to be taking her measure, maybe judging her on even the little she'd revealed.

What would he think if he knew how conflicted she felt about life in Lyndon Point—where she was always surrounded by her big, boisterous family and measured by that yardstick? Viewed through that magnifying glass?

Gabi stiffened her spine. She'd made her choices years ago after much consideration. She had nothing to apologize for. Certainly not to some hunk who worked with a bunch of cute unwanted critters.

Just then, the critter in her arms began to wriggle. In less than a nanosecond, he bailed from her clasp. "Hey, you! Get back here."

The scamp was no fool. He darted between the shelter director's legs and slipped past the cracked-open door to the building's inner workings. Gabi took off after him, embarrassment a powerful motivator. She chased her charge—*temporary* charge—into a large chamber where a cacophony of barks, yips and howls deafened her. She pulled up short.

A pang pierced her heart as she looked around at all the chain-link jails—well, *cages,* she supposed. Emotions aside, the room was lined on three walls with kennel runs, which were undeniably clean and large, but the residents still rattled the gates with the force of their efforts to escape. Or did they just want to join her, Zach and her foundling for what probably looked to them like a whole lot of hide-and-seek fun?

Oh, get a grip. Both of those thoughts were crazy. She shouldn't project her feelings, good or bad, onto the dogs. They probably were simply excited by her unexpected presence in the building. And sure, every animal wanted to run free all the time, but it could pose a real danger to a dog out on the streets. At least here at the shelter, these guys were clean and safe.

A few kennels, however, revealed shy, skittish residents huddled in a corner. Her heart went out to them. The rowdy barking was enough to drive *her* nuts, so she could only imagine how these poor, scared canines felt about the constant racket. Or maybe her oversensitivity to the noise just showed she wasn't cut out to be a dog owner, after all. Of course! That was it. The little guy she'd found would be better off in a forever home with someone else. She sighed. Somehow that didn't comfort her much. Her stray had a quite a gift. He'd known just how to worm his way into her heart.

Setting her melancholy aside, she studied the large area, her attention lingering on the various dogs. The shelter population ranged from exquisite examples of the most popular breeds—a couple of retrievers, some shelties and cocker spaniels, a cute Pomeranian, one gorgeous blue-eyed Siberian husky—all the way to a collection of the typical mixed-breeds, whose only claim to fame was the pull they exerted on the viewer's heart.

Gabi drew in a deep breath and caught the scent of good, strong disinfectant cleaner underlain with a hint of animal musk. The barking continued, the exuberance somewhat tempered but still begging for attention. She felt still another pang. In spite of the satisfactory conditions, these other guys still had no owner to play with and lavish love on them. *Yet*.

Again, yearning unfurled inside her, a longing for something just beyond her grasp. She was in no position to help these dogs any more than she could help her own stray. Which thought brought her back from her fanciful imaginings to her present dilemma. Where had the little scamp gone?

When she didn't spot her wayward charge anywhere, Gabi spun around, plunked her fists on her hips and glared at the shelter's director. "Don't just stand there…er…" What was his name? "Um… Zeke—"

"It's Zach."

To her intense annoyance, she saw the corner of

Zach's mouth twitch as though trying to widen into a smile. Her mortification grew.

She tossed her ponytail back over her shoulder in an effort to regain the dignity she'd lost the moment she stuck her head in the refrigerator back at the restaurant. And…well, a touch of the bravado she lacked, too.

"Okay, Zach. Are you going to stand there and laugh at me, or are you going to help me find your newest—what do you call them? Residents? Guests?"

He glanced at the noisy canines with a gentle smile on his lips. The evidence of his caring touched Gabi.

"They're our guests." He set down the manila folder he'd carried since he'd first walked into the shelter's waiting room and crossed his arms. "But it doesn't look like yours wants to join the others."

She shot Zach a rueful smile. "No, it doesn't. And it won't make a difference, since I don't have much choice."

He turned slowly, his gray eyes scanning the auditorium-sized room. "I know you said you have a lease issue, but what about your parents? Wouldn't they like to help you out with your new friend? After all, you did say you found him behind their business."

Gabi winced. "Any other time, I would have taken him home to Papa, but my father had a stroke four weeks ago, and his recovery has been rougher than we ever imagined. Mama's hands are full taking care of our cranky patient, who has no intention of slowing down, no matter what the doctors say."

"I'm sorry."

The warmth in his expression made Gabi's eyelids sting. She fought back the tears, knowing full well that the moment she let down her guard the floodgates would open, and then even Noah's rainstorm would pale in comparison. She didn't want to bawl like a baby in front of the most dynamic man she'd met in years.

"Yeah, me too. Thanks." She took a deep breath. "Let's see if we can catch this escape artist so I can get back to work."

"Work?" Zach dropped down on one knee to check behind a stack of white five-gallon pails near the back of the room. "I thought you said you work in Cleveland."

"I do, but I'm helping out at Tony's right now. Mama hasn't gone in since Papa had the stroke."

He glanced over his shoulder. "No wonder you looked familiar. That picture in the restaurant is you." He studied her for a moment, then he smiled. "So you're the Carlinis' Gabi. I've heard a lot about you. Everyone who meets your parents does."

The blush shot straight up to her forehead. "I'm sorry they bored you with all that stuff. No matter what, I can't get them to stop."

"Don't apologize." He stood. "My mom and dad have been gone for six and eight years now, and I miss them every day. I wouldn't mind being embarrassed by their pride every now and then, if that meant they were still around. You don't know how lucky you are."

Gabi braced against the shudder. Oh, yes. She knew.

Sure, she had some issues when it came to her family—fine, fine, more than some. Still, a surge of fear so intense it knotted her stomach, making it hard to breathe, and strong enough to almost bring her to her knees, had struck when Mama had called to tell her about Papa's stroke. Her knees had remained weak and her icy hands had shivered for hours after the phone call. Gabi had never felt so vulnerable in her life.

Antonio Carlini was gruff and a tease and as Old Country as they came, but he was also a rock, her papa. In a vague, subconscious way, she'd always known her parents were getting older, but her mother's phone call had made that reality much more real. It had shaken her that day. It still did.

But as much as she loved her folks, there were some things about their boisterous…oh…Italianness that made her crazy. That wasn't anything Zach needed to know. "Thanks—again. Anyway, no sign of the beastlet over there?"

He chuckled as he stood. "None, but let's not give

up yet. He's pretty small, and we store mountains of supplies back here. He could hide just about anywhere."

Gabi smiled back. "And we won't hear an informant ratting on him, will we?"

She peeked into the corner behind a neat stack of sealed tubs of antibacterial products but found no trace of her escapee. Then she heard a rustle and a crunch from the other side of the room, where fifty-pound sacks of kibble lay in a neat stack about ten high, looking much like a store display—supersize, of course.

She turned, grinned, brought a finger to her lips. "Listen." More crunches. "I found him. Look over there, at your mountain of dog kibble sacks."

He quirked up one corner of his mouth and pointed toward their left. "You go that way," he said in an equally quiet voice. "I'll go to the right. Maybe he's so hungry he won't hear us coming."

Gabi grinned. "The element of surprise."

"You got it." Mischief twinkled in the silver-flecked gaze. "On the count of three. One, two, three…go!"

Quickly and quietly Gabi followed his command.

The munching continued. A few feet away, she slowed, matched her steps to Zach's. The pup's hunger appeared unabated, his burger meal notwithstanding.

With her bottom lip between her teeth, she stepped

closer, hoping the fugitive didn't make himself sick eating so much so fast. Time to retrieve him, for his own good. She mouthed, *Ready?*

Zach nodded. "Grab a bag—I will, too. That'll flush him out."

They reached at the same time, yanked two sacks of kibble out of the way. The munching stopped with a startled yip. Sharp claws scrabbled against sleek concrete floor after a second of silence. Then the filthy scrap of canine darted out from the right side of the rest of the stacked bags. Zach was ready for him.

"Gotcha!" The shelter director scooped up Gabi's find, undeterred by the dog's filthy coat and strong eau de mutt scent, even though his nostrils did twitch.

"I hate to say it, but I do need to get back to Tony's." Her gaze stuck to the little dog. She wished she could—

No. She couldn't let herself think like that. For the umpteenth time, she reminded herself that she was in *no* position to adopt a stray. "What do we need to do next?"

Zach narrowed his eyes and tightened his lips. But all he said was, "Paperwork. Let me put this guy in his own guest quarters so he doesn't get away from us again, and then we can take care of the business end of things. You need to know we're about to have an adoption fair in a week's time. He'll be included in it—all the animals in the shelter at that time will be. Are you sure about this?"

Tears stung Gabi's eyes once again. No, she wasn't sure. But she had a lease to honor. And she'd built a whole life somewhere else. She was sure of that. But about the dog...

She swallowed. Hard. "I'm sure."

She hoped.

"Pretty girl, isn't she?" Oscar Worley, the shelter's most faithful volunteer, asked Zach a few minutes after Gabi Carlini had left.

"It's a he." Zach held the still-trembling new arrival close to his chest while the sink filled with warm water. "And I don't know how you can say he's *pretty*. Filthy and a ragtag assortment of dog breed parts? Yes. Cute once I wash him? Maybe. Lovable? Of course. But a pretty dog? No way."

Oscar tsk-tsked. "Never made you out for a fool, Zach. The *girl*. That girl's awfully pretty. She always has been a pretty one, with those big brown eyes and all that dark hair, ever since she was a little thing."

Even though he fought it with all his might, the blush reached up to the roots of Zach's hair. "Ah... well, I...um...paid attention to the dog. I did have a job to do."

Oscar laughed. "Fess up, now, boss. I know Gabi and I know you. She's pretty, you noticed, and it's perfectly fine if you are drawn to a girl like her. No shame in that, son. None at all."

To avoid Oscar's too-keen gaze, Zach turned off the spigot and plopped his new charge into the warm water. "Now that you mention it, okay—" The pup's yelps gave him cover, so he cut off his response. He turned to the dog but continued to glance at Oscar as he worked.

"A man could do worse, Zach," the older man said. "Much worse. She's a terrific young woman— smart, hardworking, with a heart as big as our Puget Sound." He winked. "And pretty."

Zach sent his friend a crooked grin. "I think you've said it about a dozen times, Oscar. I get your drift. But I'm the last man who's looking for a 'pretty' girl. Not right now, that's for sure. I've got a lot on my plate—too much." He cleared his throat. "Remember, I'm new around here. Lyndon Point's counting on me to put the shelter on solid footing, and that's going to take up just about all of my time. Maybe a couple of years from now I'll look around for one of these 'pretty' girls of yours. Right here in town, too, okay?"

"Just watch out, son." The older man ran a hand through his thinning white hair. "The good ones, they don't come around all that often, you know. If a man's not paying attention, some other smarter fellow will snap up the one who's walking by. Right out from under your nose."

A squirt of canine shampoo frothed into gunky brown suds on the dog's dirty coat. It was going to take multiple tries to get him clean. "That's why I'm not looking these days. Right now, my situation's not one that lends itself to dating. I can't afford the time, so I don't look. That way, the one that gets snapped up won't cause me any heartburn. I choose to focus on the dogs. And the cats."

Oscar reached for the industrial steel bucket on wheels where he'd mixed hot water and the shelter's pungent antibacterial cleaner, and headed toward the rear section of kennels. "Just make sure you don't pass up the right one just because you're still letting what's over and done with hold you back. Look around you, son. Smell the salt air. Trust God." He drew a deep breath. "Otherwise, you could wind up filling your days with a bucket and a mop just to get out of an empty, lonely house. Like me."

Zach sucked in a rough breath. He couldn't deny the wisdom in his friend's words, but although Oscar waited for a reply, he didn't answer. He knew the older man was right to a point, but he wasn't ready for a relationship. Not yet. His wounds were too raw.

And they hadn't even been inflicted by a woman.

From his perspective, a romance-gone-wrong had to be easier to overcome. His failure had been greater, went more to the core than a rough breakup ever could. He'd failed in his career, his dream. Ever since the first time he'd helped his mother knead a lump of bread at the family kitchen table, he'd dreamed of owning a restaurant, of becoming a great chef. And he'd achieved it.

For too brief a time.

No eatery, no matter how elegant or welcoming or appealing, and no chef, no matter how creative, competent or caring, could succeed if diners fell ill. As they had at his restaurant.

Salmonella had stolen in on the produce he'd bought from an upscale organic operation, borne by unsterile fertilizer. Meals he'd prepared with those beautiful but invisibly tainted vegetables had sent people to the hospital. He'd endangered their health, their lives. Any of them could have died. It was a burden Zach would bear for the rest of his days.

No. He wasn't ready to indulge in the frivolous pleasure of dating a pretty girl.

And, regardless of how Oscar saw her, Gabi Carlini was no longer a girl. She was a woman, a beautiful woman who loved dogs, in spite of her lease requirements, and pink, a color he'd always associated with sassy, lighthearted fun.

Did the association match Gabi Carlini, as well?

Chapter Three

As Gabi walked back to her parents' restaurant, she couldn't help but wonder what Zach thought of her. His steel-gray gaze had strayed toward her numerous times as she'd signed all those forms that turned the stray over to the shelter's care. While she had no idea what he thought of her, she suspected whatever opinion he held didn't much flatter her. His expressive eyes had said more than the words he'd spoken.

Of course, he didn't know her crazy family, either, the whole extended lot of them. Even if he did know her parents from eating at Tony's, which really didn't count.

Why it mattered to her so much coming from him, she didn't know. She just knew it did. Besides, she couldn't stand the thought of any more taunts about Mafia dons or corny Dean Martin songs about pizzas and moons and people's eyes. It had happened too often and with too many people. In fact, she'd had more than a bellyful of them to color her life in Lyndon Point a negative shade of embarrassment. Really, it shouldn't matter, since she wasn't likely to see him again other than to check on the dog, but the scenario had played itself out too often in her childhood and teen years.

She didn't want it to happen with Zach Davenport.

Oh, good grief. What was she thinking? She had to get back to Cleveland before she let all the ancient history affect her life again. She had to get away from Lyndon Point before her hard-gained individual identity and self-esteem retreated to high school levels. To do that, she had to get Tony's back on sure footing.

At the restaurant, Gabi put the dog and the shelter's attractive new director out of her mind and marshaled her troops. With the help of her parents' teen employees, she scrubbed, dumped, disinfected and still managed to keep the dining room open for hungry customers.

Hours flew by. Her back began to ache and Cleveland loomed even more appealing than before. She missed her routine back in Ohio, her uncomplicated life, her cute home, and especially her best friend and perennial roommate since college, Allison Stoddard.

A half hour later, on her way to the back door at Tony's yet one more time, the need to touch base with that faraway life got to her, and Gabi paused to place a call. Allie answered with a squeal, and the two women chattered as they always did, about everything and nothing, with the exuberance of close friends. She didn't, however, stop what she'd been on the way to do, but instead sandwiched her cell phone between her right ear and shoulder as she continued lugging the trash toward the door. This latest bag of iffy ingredients headed to the Dumpster felt even heavier than the others.

"You'd never believe it," she told Allie. "I'm up to my eyeballs in spoiled cheese and pizza sauce, and such close contact with a Dumpster makes it awful to breathe deep."

As she stepped out into the dingy alley, she wrinkled her nose in appreciation for Lyndon Point's fresh sea air as she prepared her approach to the trash container. "It reeks up to higher than the peak of Mount Rainier. You can't imagine how much stuff can hide in the back of a commercial cooler."

"Did anyone come down with food poisoning?" Allie asked. "It sounds like you have the—ahem!—perfect recipe there."

"Whoa, don't even go there, woman!" Gabi gave her load another tug. "We dodged a bullet on that account." She explained what had happened. "Fortunately," she added, "the kids my parents employ served the stuff in the front of the fridge, so no one got sick. When I opened the cooler and started to move things around, though, I caught a funky whiff, and that sent me digging. That's when I found the expired ingredients. But food poisoning? That spells death for a restaurant."

Gabi dropped the weighty sack to grab her phone. "Hang on a sec. I need both hands to get this trash bag into the Dumpster." Moments later, she wiped her hands on the seat of her shorts and picked up her cell again. "I'm back."

Allie went on. "Why don't you just close down the place, if it's in such bad shape?"

"Because Mama and Papa—"

"I just love how you say their names, with that Italian accent. It's so…I don't know. Old Country… Tuscan…cultured European."

"Oh, stop."

That was all she needed. For even Allie to see her as Old Country. That was her family, not her.

Still, Gabi couldn't deny she'd always thought of her parents by the old-fashioned names. She doubted she could change, since it happened spontaneously, even now. The best thing for her to do was change the subject.

"Anyway," she said, her voice firm, her tone deliberate, "my parents can't pay insurance premiums or co-pays if money doesn't come in. The bills from Dad's stroke could clear the national debt."

With her usual lack of tact, Allie plowed on. "Then put your years of experience to good use and find yourself a chef and a manager, so you can hustle back here to Cleveland. Damon's not happy about your absence."

Damon Schuler, Gabi's boss, wasn't endowed with patience. "I have four weeks of saved vacation plus another three of personal time. He can handle the office. For goodness' sake, he's the one who started the business."

Allie snickered. "When I stopped there for the files you asked me to get, he had his tie flipped over a shoulder, glasses at the tip of his nose, and his hair looked like a bird's nest."

Gabi managed the Cleveland office of Damon's Executive Placements firm, and before leaving, she'd been converting the hard-copy files of the office's most high-powered executive clients to digital format. She'd asked Allie to ship those files to Lyndon Point, and planned to catch up in the evenings after she'd finished at Tony's.

"Oh, please," she said, using more oomph than she felt. "Did he forget he used to run things before the business grew so big he had to open satellite offices in other states? Of course, he can do it. If not, he can get his wife to help. Irene managed the office before they married."

"Great minds think alike! When he complained about you abandoning him to all your work, I suggested a temp, but he countered with something about Irene claiming she's forgotten everything in the twenty years since she left." She hesitated. "Then he mentioned a Wilma and Florida, and ushered me out of his office. He did sound upset. And who's Wilma?"

Guilt fought Gabi's common sense. "Wilma took over after Irene. She retired to Florida when I started. Besides, whose side are you on—Damon's or mine?"

"I'm on mine. I want my roomie back."

"Believe me, I'm not crazy about being back in my hometown, but I can't leave. Papa's stroke was serious, and Mama won't leave him for a second. He's not debilitated enough for a nursing home, but he has to learn to use the wheelchair, and can't care for himself yet. Therapy should get him there, but it's been only a month since..."

"I know." Allie's voice softened. "I'm just being a brat—sorry. I do understand and would do the same if it was Dad."

Allie's mother had died of complications from diabetes their junior year in college. Father and daughter had grown closer than ever in the ensuing years.

Gabi stood and grasped the doorknob. "I should have come home as soon as Mama called that first night, but I foolishly let her talk me into postponing my return. If only I'd been here sooner, I could have kept Tony's from becoming such a mess."

"And if wishes were fishes—what is that cliché? I know there is one."

"Beats me. I'm just a business major—*you're* the teacher." She sighed. "Anyway, gotta go. This place needs me more right now than you need me back there. Or Damon."

Her parents needed her. She was there for them, no matter what. No matter how much her memories of growing up in Lyndon Point rattled her. No matter what the great-looking guy at the animal shelter might think of her.

At nine forty-five that night, Gabi walked into the house, more exhausted than she'd felt in years, But she didn't have the luxury of taking time off, since she had to keep the restaurant afloat for her parents' sakes. She went to her room, grabbed clean shorts and a T-shirt and hit the shower to wash off the grime of the day. Clean again, she walked down the stairs and to the kitchen. She made a beeline to the refrigerator for an icy can of root beer. Mama always stocked up when she knew Gabi was coming home. As she popped the tab, a note on the table caught her attention.

Her parents had gone to bed already, her mother wrote, and would see her in the morning. The translated message spoke of her mother's expectation of Gabi's detailed account of things at Tony's. But how could she do that? If either of her parents knew how she'd found the place, they'd insist on running it themselves again. That would be devastating for her father. He was in no condition to work. Not yet.

Maybe never again—

No! She couldn't think that way. His doctors had said Antonio Carlini would recover, and they expected him to return to work soon enough. True, he might never put in twelve hours a day like he had in the past, but they believed he should be able to spend a decent amount of time making the pizzas, calzones and pastas he loved to serve his faithful customers.

If he gave his body the chance to recover.

"Oh, Lord," she said on a sigh. "Bless him with Your strength, cradle him in the palm of Your healing hand."

Of course, she couldn't tell Mama or Papa what she'd found in that kitchen. Besides, while cleaning out the fridge, a germ of an idea had popped into her thoughts and found fertile soil in her imagination. Soon she'd seen the restaurant in a different light.

Now she was sure that with her business know-how, she could help her parents upgrade Tony's. If, instead of the kitschy pizza place it always had been, she were to turn it into a chic and elegant Italian bistro, surely they'd see reason. She felt certain positive change would inspire them to leave behind some of their more outdated ways. Then, if her parents led by example, maybe some of her other relatives would follow. Maybe the whole *famiglia* would see that toning things down a notch was the way to go. Never mind that Tony's would make a lot more money in the process, with an upscale menu and an upmarket appeal. Those medical bills loomed enormous in Gabi's mind, just as they did in her parents' minds.

She pulled out a chair, kicked off her flip-flops and sat down to enjoy her root beer. As always, Mama had dimmed the lights in the kitchen, leaving enough illumination so no one would trip if they came down for a midnight snack or something to drink. Still, the low light let Gabi look around and appreciate the warmth and cozy appeal of the efficient space.

Her parents had bought their home when she was small, before property in the coastal areas just outside of Seattle, like nearby Edmonds and in Lyndon Point, had grown prohibitive. True, the house had been practically a wreck back then, but with equal amounts of elbow grease and love, the large Cape Cod–style white cottage had become a jewel. Even the kitchen.

These days, the cabinets were a glossy white, easy to clean and bright even on the Pacific Northwest's dreariest days. Red-and-white-checked curtains framed the windows, a cheery echo of the red-and-white checkerboard-tile floor. A sprinkling of Mama's red tchotchkes, her red apron, four sassy red canisters and Papa's outrageous cookie jar—

an enormous white rooster with a scarlet comb—
turned the place into the whimsical family hub it
had always been.

She smiled. This was the room that came to mind
whenever she thought of home. Even though she'd
tried, she'd been unable to replicate its feeling in
the kitchen of the bungalow she and Allie shared in
Cleveland, and that failure drove her crazy at times,
since she'd tried so hard to get it right. The cabinets
were almost identical in style and color, the curtains
yellow-and-white checked, and she and her roommate had spent a whole lot of time shopping for
the abundance of clever blue-and-yellow accesso-
ries they'd arranged around the room. It was a very
pretty kitchen, perfect in every concrete aspect, but
even so, that missing something-or-other eluded her.

It needed something special, something that gave
it life.

Before she could stop it, the image of the stray
jelled in her thoughts. How sweet it would be to have
his company right then, to have him snuggle into
the curve of her neck again. Gabi could almost hear
the sound his claws would make against the kitchen
floor as he trotted close.

A knot formed in her throat, and she wondered
how the rascal was doing. The urge to hold him
again made her sadder than she could have expected.

"You can call to check up on him," Zach had said
before she'd left. "The phone here is connected to

my cell, so I can be reached whenever anyone finds a stray animal. You can call me anytime."

The memory of the shelter director's words was swiftly followed by the awareness of the lights she'd noticed on in the building when she'd walked past it about a half hour earlier. Was Zach Davenport still there? Would he really answer if she called?

She pulled out the business card he'd given her from the pocket of the clean cutoffs she'd put on after her shower. She stared at it, the need to know growing greater by the minute. Her stomach tightened with apprehension—and a touch of anticipation, too—as she dialed the number on the card. "Hello?" he said after the third ring.

She drew in a breath. "Hi…Zach? It's Gabi. Gabriella Carlini. I dropped off a stray earlier today."

It occurred to her to check the red-and-white clock above the stove. Almost ten o'clock. Oh, great. What nutcase called this late just to check on a dog she couldn't keep?

Obviously, a nutcase like her.

"Gabi…?"

Her breath caught in her throat at the sound of his voice. She barely knew him, but Zach Davenport was a man who left a lasting impression.

She fought to keep her own voice from rising to a higher pitch than normal. "Yes, um…"

Silence came over the line. Then he cleared his throat. "How can I help you, Gabi?"

That voice…that rich tenor voice. A random thought crossed her jumbled mind. Did he sing? She suspected he'd be good—

"Ah…Gabi?"

She blinked. "Yes…well, I, uh, wondered how the little guy has settled in. And I saw the lights still on inside the shelter on my way home. Besides, you'd said the phone would ring directly to you, so I could call whenever. So, um, that's what I did."

Oh, no. She sounded like a blubbering fool. She shook herself to try and get it together. "How is he doing? Did someone adopt him?" She held her breath waiting for his response.

Which didn't come. The seconds ticked by.

"Zach?" she asked.

The silence continued. Then he coughed. "Well, you see, it appears we have a, uh, small problem."

Uh-oh. "A problem?"

"It appears your little buddy has…well, escaped."

"No!" Gabi's stomach tightened into rock. "I can't believe this. You couldn't have been so careless with him—"

"No one was careless. If you'd let me explain—"

"It better be a good explanation." This couldn't be happening. To think she'd trusted his shelter—him—with a live creature. And then he'd lost it. "You assured me you'd find him a good home. Losing him doesn't fit that description."

Again, he hesitated. "After we bathed him, we

realized he has a lot of terrier in him. They're great diggers, especially the smaller terrier breeds like the Westies, the Cairns and the Jack Russells. Because of that terrier instinct, your buddy decided to dig his way out by going under the fence around his run. He's so small it couldn't have taken much time or effort to make a big enough hole."

"But you just said you realized he was a digging breed. Why didn't you put him in some kind of cage?"

"All our guests have a *run*. They need exercise, a place to—er, well, *go* that's separate from their den—their sleeping quarters. And besides, we're required to provide it. Besides, I did check the fence. It was secure to the ground. He dug—deep."

Gabi remembered the dog trembling, and anxiety swamped her. "Have you looked for him?"

"Of course. You saw the lights here at the building. I've been searching for the past hour, everywhere on our property and the neighborhood around us. Haven't seen even a sign of him. Still, I suppose it's better that you know what's happened."

She shouldn't be this upset. Once she'd relinquished the dog into the shelter's custody she had no further claim on him, not even on the kind or quality of care he received. The shelter and, by extension, its director, were now responsible for the animal's welfare, not her. But in Zach's voice she identified an echo of her concern, and that comforted her despite the crummy incident. She came to a quick decision, following her heart.

"Look, I'm getting Papa's big flood-sized flashlight and coming to help you look." She rummaged under the sink. "Aha! Here it is. Two sets of eyes are better than one, you know, especially where this little sneak is concerned."

She held her breath, hoping he'd agree—and not just for the dog's sake. She didn't want to admit it, but deep inside she was curious about Zach, more now that she'd heard the worry resonate in his words. She wouldn't mind seeing him again.

Even though she shouldn't care one way or the other.

She wondered what he thought of her. First, she'd shown up dirty and stinky, bearing an equally dirty and stinky stray. Then, like some overprotective mommy, she'd called to check up on the dog she'd relinquished. To him.

Did he think she had questions about his competence? Did he think she doubted his ability to care for the dog?

More important, did she doubt him?

"Are you sure? I mean, it makes sense, two of us looking," he said. "But it is late, and you must be tired."

Was that a hint of relief in his voice? Even if she had inserted her feelings into her interpretation, she made up her mind. She headed for the living room, Mama's old kitchen cordless phone between her shoulder and ear, flashlight in hand. "Yes, I'm sure. I'll meet you at the shelter, and then we can decide what to do next."

Without giving Zach an opportunity to object, she said goodbye, dropped the phone on the small console table by the front door and let herself out. The brisk night breeze off the Sound felt good against her face, its balmy touch a pleasant reminder to treasure it, since the capricious Pacific Northwest rains could change things in a flash. The salty tang of the sea tickled her nostrils, and she savored the familiar sense of coming home. The faint echo of the night's last Edmonds Ferry horn's blast traveled miles toward her in the quiet hush. Lyndon Point was a gorgeous place, with unique scenes and sounds that tempted the senses to a smorgasbord of experiences.

Ten minutes later, she rapped her knuckles against the locked door of the shelter. Footsteps approached.

"Ready?" she asked when Zach opened up.

As attractive as the shelter director had looked in his scrubs earlier that day, he was even more so in a royal-blue polo shirt and jeans. His hair was rumpled, as though he'd run his fingers through it more than once, and his eyes gleamed with a touch of blue, probably reflected from his shirt. She paused a moment and took in his masculine good looks.

"Let me lock up." He pocketed the key, then turned to Gabi. "Like I told you, I've already searched the yards in the surrounding neighbor-hood, and I also checked with 911 dispatch. No dogs turned in, and no accidents involving dogs reported tonight, no dogs seen on the loose for them to no-tify Animal Control."

She let out a sigh of relief. "I'm so glad. What do you suggest?"

"Terriers are strong-willed, determined canines. It occurred to me he might have decided to make his way back to where you first saw him, to the alley. I would have gone on my own—was about to leave, but…"

In the light of the streetlamp at the corner, Gabi saw his cheekbones redden. A sheepish expression spread over his attractive features.

As he drew out his silence, she prodded. "But…?"

"When I heard you on the phone, I wondered if he might not respond better to you than to me. He could have hidden in any of the yards I checked, but he might not trust me enough to let me see him, much less catch him. It was easy to see how much he liked you."

She smiled, remembering how she'd felt when the little rough tongue had lapped at her hand. "Well, then, what are we waiting for?"

They set off at a quick pace, giving the vicin-ity of the shelter another quick search, and arrived at Tony's a short while later. Dim light from the streetlamp three buildings away mottled the alley.

Angular shadows, deep and dark, turned the usually innocuous space into something reminiscent of horror movies. Gabi shuddered, her imagination conjuring scenes from silly films she'd watched as a teen, and which she now wished she hadn't.

Mama had been right. They'd led to nightmares, even waking ones.

Oh, good grief. How crazy could she get? Scared of shadows in the alley.

As she shook herself to shed the strange mood, she heard rustling near the far end of the alley, daunting in the night.

She glanced at Zach, who bobbed his chin toward the darker depths. She stepped up to the Dumpster, then dropped down to her knee. "Hey, um—" She looked over her shoulder at her companion. "What do I call him? Did you guys name him?"

He shook his head. "Didn't have a chance. We do give our guests temporary names to make things easier for us while they're at our facility. I can't stand to call an animal by something so stark and cold as a number. But you only brought him in a few hours ago."

"Okay, then." She scooted closer to the metal trash container, the source of the bad smells that filled the alley, wrinkling her nose as she drew near. "Hey, little guy. I'm back. Did you come to look for me?"

Nothing.

She remembered how he'd listened to her chatter earlier that day. She kept up a running conversation, hoping he would respond that way again. "Did you come for the trash? Are you hungry again?"

Behind her, Zach snorted, more than likely a smothered laugh.

She chuckled, too. "You did have a feast at the shelter, buddy, so I don't think you came back for the food. Is this where someone dumped you? Do you have a hidey-hole somewhere out here in the dark?"

Gabi continued to croon, inching closer to the Dumpster, dreading what she might find instead of a dog. Fat rats a-mocking pranced through her thoughts.

Then, in the quiet of the night, she heard the faintest of whimpers. It came from the rear corner of the steel container. "Please wait," she told Zach. "Let me go first. I'll let you know if I need you."

"Sounds good to me."

With a prayer on her lips, Gabi set the flashlight on the ground, then crept slowly on hands and knees, quiet and careful. Inches from the corner, she saw the gleam of the dog's bright eyes.

"There you are." To her surprise, he didn't back away, but neither did he come toward her. He did whine softly.

She continued her approach. "You can't stay out here, you know. It's really not safe."

Gabi didn't want to think about the threats the

pup might face in an empty alley. The image of a large tomcat crossed her mind. One of those could do the small escape artist a lot of harm. Some toms got up to as much as twenty-five pounds. She'd be surprised if this terrier mix weighed thirteen.

She held her hand about an inch away from his nose. "Come on, pal. Let's get going and get you somewhere safe."

That's when she got a good look at the dog's situation. It appeared he'd gotten wedged between the Dumpster and the building's back wall, a solid cement expanse. No wonder he'd whimpered. As much as he loved his freedom, this kind of captivity had to terrify him.

"I need your help," she told Zach. "I'm not sure how we're going to get him out of where he is. Please hand me the flashlight."

Although she knew the bright light would blind the dog, it couldn't be helped. She needed to illuminate the area. Maybe after they had a better view of the whole picture they could come up with a solution.

Zach handed her the light but didn't back away. For a moment, Gabi froze. His presence at her back was undeniable. His warmth enveloped her, and his breath wafted past her cheek. He was close, very close. She'd never been so aware of another person before.

The dog whimpered again.

"Hang on, buddy." Gabi swallowed hard as she redirected her attention to the matter at hand. She aimed the flashlight toward the dog. "This might be uncomfortable for a minute, but I can't help it. Let's see what we can do for you."

With the help of the light, Gabi and Zach soon realized the container leaned at a slender angle away from the wall, wider toward the top than down where the dog was stuck. Gabi handed Zach the light while she eased the little guy to freedom.

"There!" She sat back on her heels and nuzzled the dog. "You poor thing." The pleasant scent of cleanliness met her nose. "Oh! You washed him."

At her side, Zach chuckled. "He needed it. He was a mess."

"And then he got himself into a different kind of mess out here." She flashed him a smile. "Thanks."

He shrugged and smiled back. "I thought your help would improve our chances of catching him, so thank *you*." He tipped his head to the side. "Are you sure you really want to surrender him?"

"He has to go back to the shelter with you." She blinked hard against the sudden tears stinging her eyes.

With nothing more to say, they sat in awkward silence, the stray who'd brought them together on Gabi's lap. Seconds ticked by.

Her awareness grew.

Again.

She met Zach's gaze. Couldn't look away.

What was this…this crackle between them all about? Why him? And why now? Here in Lyndon Point?

Chapter Four

Gabi wearily pressed the palms of her hands against her eyes. She'd spent the past three hours sorting through three shoe boxes full of receipts. Funny how it had taken an hour per box.

Funny? Yeah, right. There was absolutely nothing amusing about this whole situation.

She'd never expected to find the business records of Tony's in such a shambles. Worse still, after sorting and separating, adding and even more subtracting, she now had tangible proof that the restaurant's financial outlook wasn't particularly stellar. Costs had gone way up with the price of ingredients sky-high in the tough economy, and people weren't eating out as much as they had even as recently as a few years earlier. Something had to be done to improve the fiscal picture or her parents would be in serious trouble.

And she was the woman to do it. The trick would

be for her to find a way to convey that truth to Mama and then not let Papa find out where things really stood. It wasn't the best time to alarm him, to say the least.

Gabi squared her shoulders. "Mama! Can you come to the kitchen for a minute? I've a couple of questions for you."

Questions, and a whole lot more.

"Sono qui," her mother answered. Lively steps rang out on the stairs, and a moment later she walked into the cheery kitchen. "I'm here," she repeated, then went straight to the counter, where the coffeemaker always held at least half a pot full of rich, dark brew, to pour herself a steaming hot cup. "What you want to know?"

"Have you looked at—" she waved at the receipts "—all this?"

Mama took a long drink of her coffee, set the cup down carefully on the matching saucer, then sighed, never once letting her near-black eyes meet Gabi's gaze. "No. You know your Papa always does this. He and your *cugino* Ryder take care of accounts." As though for emphasis, she shook her head, making her short, graying curls bounce.

Gabi fought back a snicker. Calling Lyndon Point's mayor, Ryder Lyndon, her cousin was stretching family ties a tad far. While the two of them had grown up as the closest of friends, Ryder was actually the son of Mama's second cousin who—

knows-how-many-times-removed. He didn't even refer to her parents as aunt or uncle. But then, her family was all about…well, family. Sometimes— often—too much.

"This time," she said, serious, "you don't get a choice. Papa can't take care of the business end of things any more than he can run the kitchen. You and I are the ones who have to take up the slack."

Mama's gaze flew to the window over the sink, and Gabi didn't miss the shuddery breath she inhaled. "But he's better now. Soon, he can—"

"No, he can't. Not yet, not for a while, and you know it."

She hated to push, aware how much it would upset her mother, but she had no choice. As long as she was in Lyndon Point she could take on the management, including the bookkeeping and accounting, of the pizzeria. But before she left, and she would as soon as she could, she had to have someone in charge. Mama had run the dining room like a smoothly oiled machine for years, and at all of fifty-two, she was nowhere near too old to handle the expanded responsibilities—no matter how she tried to avoid work she didn't feel suited her talents. After all, these weren't normal times.

Although Gabi didn't doubt her mother's capability for even one moment, her mother had taken advantage of Papa's insistence on pampering her over the years. But this couldn't be circumvented. He needed them to step up.

"You do want to help Papa, don't you?"

Mama sighed. "Yes, but—"

"Good," Gabi cut in. "So here's the deal. I have a good idea what we need to do to turn this around. For one, we have to be careful with costs—"

"Bah! Everything too expensive all the time now. How they want people to live, every time a dollar more here, ten more there?"

Oops! That hadn't been where she'd intended the conversation to go. "Um, yes, and that's why we have to be smarter than the economy. It means we need to make a few…ah…adjustments. I have some ideas that should help."

Mama turned back to her, eyes narrowed. "Ideas?"

"Yes, ideas. We can adjust things a little and jump on current trends. I think we could tweak Tony's a little and turn it into the perfect Italian bistro. Bistros are everywhere, and doing very well. If we did that, we would bring in customers from Seattle, and we wouldn't have to count only on Lyndon Point residents. They can only eat a steady amount of pizza."

"Bistro? *Seattle?*"

From her mother's tone of voice, one would think Seattleites were nigh unto Venutians or something. This wasn't the way Gabi had hoped her suggestion would be received. Before she could press her point, though, her mother scoffed.

"Bah! Tony's is pizzeria, not bistro. It does fine."

Gabi turned her notebook toward Mama. "Not so fine these days. Take a look at the numbers. We're barely making a profit after you pay all the bills. Papa's medical costs are high, and they could wipe you out if we don't change something."

Her mother gave the pages nothing more than a brief glance and a dismissive wave. "But—"

"You know what I'm talking about, Mama," she said. "Remember that TV show you like so much? The one where the restaurant expert walks into a place that's about to go under, changes everything that's wrong, and then opens it up again, only better? That's what we need to do with Tony's."

A momentary hesitation told her Mama at least was thinking about it. Then she said, "Tony's not failing, Gabriella. We no need the Brit. *È troppo*—too much, that is. We do make money like we are."

"Nowhere near enough to keep you and Papa going." She tapped the open notebook with her index finger. "Here. You have to take the time and look at this. Carefully."

As her mother read the figures, the color in her face vanished. She shook her head slowly as she continued to stare. Then she snapped the notebook shut and met Gabi's gaze, her jaw firm, her shoulders stiff.

"Fine. Change what you want, but not Tony's. It's a pizzeria. Always was."

Before Gabi could come to grips with that kind of logic—or lack thereof—Mama stood and marched away, mumbling something about it being time for Papa's medicine.

Frustrated, she collapsed back into the kitchen chair. Now what?

Reality hadn't changed, even though her mother had said she could change whatever she wanted. But what could she really do, since in her next breath, Mama had put the brakes on any meaningful change?

Where did she go from here? "Lord…? Is Mama in denial or just stubborn? I think I know what I have to do, but help me out, please. Show me how to reach her, how to win her over to my way of seeing things. Or they could face financial disaster in no time at all."

The more Gabi thought about the situation, the more clearly she saw only one way out. Change had to happen. Even Mama had recognized that. But the only way to make a significant difference would be if Gabi moved forward with her ideas. Mama would see how much better everything was once the changes were made. Wouldn't she?

Sure, she would.

After all, Gabi was the one who'd done all kinds of traveling in the past five years. She'd seen a whole lot more of the country during those trips than her mother had in twenty years or more. She knew best.

Calling up all her courage, she came to a decision. She was going to forge ahead. Even after Mama's declaration. Her parents needed it. They needed her to rescue them.

"Zach!" Claudia called from the waiting room of the shelter. "Just talked to Ryder. He's got the permits ready to go for the street. The Adoption Fair's jelling into place with every minute that goes by."

He didn't look up from the shelter's latest rescue. This one had been brought in with a severe skin condition due to months of neglect of her coat and hygiene, rotten teeth and diabetes. He needed to trim off the worst knots in the matted hair to keep the clippers from pulling too hard when he gave the sad little girl the much-needed buzz cut.

"Have you notified all our foster families?" he asked.

"Letters went out last week," his right-hand woman answered from the doorway where she now stood. "Email alerts out yesterday, and I plan to call them all the day before the event. That should do it. They should all be at the fair to show off their fosters."

"Sounds good." He leaned closer to the stray to look at the hot spot he'd discovered. Poor thing had to be going crazy from the itch and pain. Once he cut off all the tangles that pulled at the root of the hair, she should be able to heal.

Satisfied with his inspection, if not happy with the dog's condition, he glanced up at Claudia. "Did you ask the foster families to get the word out to their friends and neighbors? We need forever homes for these guys. Just look at this one."

Claudia knelt at his side, her prematurely pewter hair falling in a sleek cascade close to the dog. She grabbed it back with one hand, and let the rescue lick her other hand.

"If I didn't already have five of my own, I'd take her home with me tonight."

He shook his head. "Ha! Don't even think of it. I like Rick, and don't want to get on his wrong side." He grinned at the thought of the burly navy officer. "Your husband's no pushover, you know? Those muscles don't bode well for me if I do. Besides, I remember him telling you no more strays after the last adoption."

Standing, she laughed. "Don't give me that weakling routine. You're no slouch, yourself, boss. I've seen you keep right up with Rick on that canoe, and let's not forget you beat his socks off when we went skiing. About the adoptions, he's said no more of them ever since the first one. Just like he said no more kids after the first one."

Zack arched an eyebrow. "I didn't know that. I guess you must have been the one with the…oh, let's call them wishes for *abundance*. Five of each is a far shot from no more than one."

She shrugged, a mischievous grin brightening her smooth, copper-colored skin. "He saw the light after I invested in a lot of prayer, and a whole lot of talking was done."

"You're stubborn."

"Just persuasive."

The front door's motion sensor chimed, alerting them to the arrival of a potential rescuer. "Gotta get back to work," she said. "I hear the boss around here is a tyrant."

"Get out of here," he said, laughing. "You run this place more than I do." With the lightest touch, he picked up the hurting dog and placed her on the grooming table in the middle of the room.

As he worked on her coat, he couldn't stop thoughts of his last rescue from entering his mind. Gabi Carlini's terrier mix was one special character. The pup had stolen the hearts of everyone at the shelter with his antics and sweet nature. Still, he kept trying to escape at every turn, even after the shelter staff had fortified his kennel to where the thing rivaled Lyndon Point's Animal Control truck.

At the oddest moment, they would find him either in the storage room gnawing at the sacks of kibble or stuck under the latest addition to the chain-link fence around his outside run. He was one determined little guy, all right.

Brought in by one determined woman. Gabi had called every single day since the night of the great escape, just to check on her rescue. Zach knew she didn't intend to keep the pup, but in his mind, he was hers. The dog seemed to agree with Zach.

As soon as she'd appear at the shelter to visit him, the terrier would dance and bark with more enthusiasm than any other dog in the shelter had displayed to date. As soon as he was set free, he jumped à la hoops star, bounding around Gabi until she picked him up and hugged him. Then he returned the favor by licking her face all over.

That dog was hers, no matter what she said.

And she was that dog's human. No matter what she said.

Anyone could see it. She lit up as soon as she saw the little rascal and even more when she cuddled and played with him as though she'd owned him from birth. Although shelter policy mandated the guests be kept leashed during any and all visits, the escape artist showed no interest in going anywhere but to Gabi's side when she showed up. Zach suspected they could have gotten away without the leash.

Maybe. He was a terrier, after all. Zach wasn't about to test the well-known terrier bolting instinct, at any rate.

As he reached for the clippers, he heard a familiar voice out front. At the same time, an equally familiar volley of barks sounded from the kennel side of the building. Gabi had arrived, and her dog knew it.

Even though he shouldn't, he scooped up the new stray, who'd been shaking since he'd set her on the grooming table, and held her close as he returned her to her kennel. It wouldn't hurt her to relax a little and, instead, would help her handle the upcoming ordeal much better.

And if he told himself that enough times maybe he'd convince himself he was being strictly altruistic here. Truth was that while it *would* benefit the anxious dog to calm down before going through the extensive grooming, he wanted to see Gabi again. She didn't draw only her rescue—she also drew Zach, like a steak did a starving stray.

As soon as his charge had curled up on the hammock-like bed in her kennel, he shook off the worst of the dog hair from his blue scrubs and hurried to the kennel side. He found her inside the playroom, where potential adoptive families had the opportunity to interact with the hopeful adoptees.

"Hey there," he said as he closed the door behind him. "How's your buddy doing today?"

She arched a graceful brow. "My buddy? He's not mine, but yours—temporarily." She turned away from Zach and stared out the room's glass wall, as he'd noticed she did every time either one of them mentioned the stray's ownership situation. "He's going to be a hit at the Adoption Fair."

Zach tamped down the flare of irritation. "He

sure is, and he'll soon have his own family loving him like he deserves."

Although she tried to hide it, he saw her wince. "Yeah, that is what he really does need." She swallowed hard, squeezed the furry toy in her hand to catch the terrier's attention and then turned to face Zack. "How are the arrangements for the event going? Is everything all set up?"

"Pretty close. Claudia just heard from the mayor. He signed off on closing the street for the day."

"Oh, wow! You really plan to do this up, don't you?"

"I'd like to turn it into a seasonal thing, but I have to prove it'll be a plus for the town. This is only the first one for us."

"Sure, but I also know Mr. Mayor quite well." She grinned. "Ryder's a lifelong friend, and even my six-degrees-of-separation distant cousin. He's not dumb. Once he sees how well this goes, he'll jump right on the bandwagon with you. If he hasn't already."

"Well, he signed off on everything I needed."

She raised her shoulders and grinned. "Told ya."

Zack was charmed. He couldn't tear his gaze away from her sparkling eyes and animated features as she played fetch with the dog. It wasn't just her natural beauty that drew him. Gabi Carlini radiated a vibrancy he'd never encountered before.

Even her thick, wavy hair seemed to bounce with that same energy.

He crossed his arms. "Tell me. Am I wrong, or have you been here every single day since you brought him in?"

A rosy tint brightened her cheeks, and she tossed the end of her ponytail over her shoulder. "Um... pretty much." She jammed her hands into her khaki shorts pockets, then gave him a narrow-eyed stare, a mock-stern expression on her face. "I want to make sure you're doing your job. Gotta do some quality control where my foundling's concerned, you know?"

Zach struggled to hide a wince. Anytime anyone brought up mention of doing a job right and quality control, his skin felt itchy. The memories of his restaurant were still too raw and close to the surface, and quality...well, it wasn't always as easy to control as one would think.

He ran a hand through his hair. "We do try to do our best here, and I think we succeed."

She glanced back through the room's glass wall and down the aisle of cages, clean and well kept, as he tried to maintain them at all times. "I'd say your best is excellent. There are some real horror stories out there about animal shelters."

A flare of irritation burst inside him. "Don't believe everything you read. I've volunteered at shelters ever since I was in junior high. Can't even remember how many of them by now. I've never been in one that resembled any of the atrocities you read about in the media. I know the bad ones exist, but not all are bad."

"Whoa! I'm sorry. I didn't mean to offend you. I'm glad you've had such great experiences over the years. Is that why you decided to go into— Are you a vet?"

Great. This was going from bad to worse really fast. "Uh...no. I'm just someone who loves animals, have done every kind of job a shelter could throw at me, and found I was good at running one."

She didn't reply right away, and he cringed. Now that he thought of it, his explanation sounded really lame. What kind of idiot just sort of bumbles out of career disaster and into running an animal shelter?

A failed gourmet chef and restaurateur kind of idiot, that's who. He sighed. "Well, it was great to see you again. I have a new intake who needs a whole lot of attention. See you soon."

Out of the corner of his eye, he saw her confusion. And who could blame her? They'd been talking like perfectly normal people, and then *bam!* He'd cut her right off.

"Yeah, see ya." She picked up the squeak toy again. As he stepped out of the room, however, he saw her glance his way again. "Bye."

Did he imagine it, or was she as reluctant to say goodbye as he was?

Nah. Couldn't be. She was a kind, decent person and he was damaged.

He hurried toward the utility half of the building, wishing things might be different. Then he would've…

What *would* he have said to the very unsettling Gabriella Carlini?

Dumb. Dumb, dumb, dumb.

Why on earth had she gone back to the shelter? Why couldn't she stay away?

The dog.

She really got a kick out of the stray, but she had to be honest. She'd wanted to see more than the little terrier. She'd wanted to see the shelter director, too.

Zach Davenport was a very attractive man. And more than just in looks. The way he cared for those animals was unexpectedly endearing. A man with such a heart was one Gabi couldn't resist.

And she hadn't really been trying to resist him. Even though she should. Gabi had to remember she was in Lyndon Point only to right the sinking ship otherwise known as Tony's Pizzeria. She couldn't afford to let her emotions get tangled up with the shelter, much less the shelter's director.

"You're here to turn the restaurant into a chic, gourmet Italian eatery," she reminded herself as she marched back to Tony's. "And to move Mama and Papa's way of doing things into the twenty-first century."

To accomplish any of that, she had to focus all her attention on stopping the restaurant's downhill slide rather than on the intriguing man she'd just left. The sooner she had everything cleaned up and headed toward a better future, the sooner she could return to her *real* life, her job and her hard-won independence.

"And don't you forget it," she muttered.

As she said the words, however, her traitorous brain brought the handsome shelter director back into her thoughts. The one place where she couldn't ignore him. So what was going on with Zach? Why had he morphed from the laughing man she liked to the moody stranger she didn't care for nearly as much? After all, he'd been the one to come to see her as she'd played with the dog.

True, she'd expected Zach to do so, since he'd spent time talking to her every time she'd gone to the shelter, but she hadn't expected him to turn from sunshine and rainbows to dark skies and thunder.

Maybe it was for the best that he had. Otherwise, she might be in danger of letting her attraction to him grow into something a whole lot more risky than it already was. She couldn't let that happen. She couldn't let her heart get drawn into his appeal.

She had to get back to Cleveland before all the strides she'd made in the past few years went down the proverbial drain.

Chapter Five

By lunchtime the next day, a brilliant idea had struck Gabi. At least, she thought it was brilliant. It would give her a perfectly good reason to go to the shelter and see the terrier. And she wouldn't even have to see the director.

After all, what guy could resist fresh, free pizza? While he was busy eating, she'd be happy playing with the pup.

And by coincidence, a pair of everything-goes Garbage Pies sat on the steel table in the kitchen. After the waitress had brought the order to the table, the customer had realized Garbage Pies included not only every kind of meat on Tony's menu, but also every veggie in the place. They'd only wanted the meats, so they'd sent their original order back in exchange for Multi-Meat pies.

"Hey, Dylan," she said, the reject pizzas packed in white delivery boxes with Tony's red-and-green logo printed across the top. "I'm going to visit the puppy. Since these two canceled orders are just sitting here, I'll take them to the shelter staff. We still have a medium olive-and-jalapeño and half a Hawaiian pie hanging around back here, too. You guys can eat those, right? Please?"

"Love the jalapeños, boss! But—" he jabbed a thumb over his shoulder "—that crazy Mandy, she likes pineapple on her pies." He shook his head. "Can't explain some people's bad taste."

"Huh?" the teenage waitress shot back. "Those fiery green things don't belong on Italian food. They're Mexican, remember? So who's the one with the lousy taste now?"

Gabi laughed. "Just make sure you guys eat it all. I don't want it to go to waste, and ever since I made her look over the accounts, Mama's been on the warpath about costs. You don't want to incur her wrath."

"Don't worry," Dylan said, snagging a slice loaded with peppers and rubbing his nonexistent belly with his other hand. "If there's one thing I'm good at, it's eating."

"Life is just so good." Mandy drew out her every syllable in pure bliss. "Who'd ever think your boss would order you to eat pizza at work?"

Gabi chuckled again as she walked out of Tony's, but grew serious soon enough. True, most people loved pizza, but that business plan wasn't cutting it for them these days. She was taking steps to put the place on a better path, and that now hinged on her recruiting a top chef or a restaurant manager. More likely, she'd need both. Once she nailed that, she'd make sure the new hires ran the new venture smoothly. And made money, too, of course, since her plan was to invest every cent she'd saved since she'd graduated college. Her parents' future was worth it.

A touch of dread slammed her gut. She feared she might have a fight on her hands if her parents realized what she'd done after she implemented the changes but before the results were in. Still, it had to happen. Then, too, it wouldn't be just them who'd object. Her extended family would, no doubt, be furious with her and oppose everything she tried. Well, they would until they saw the positive outcome.

She hoped.

But she'd have to worry about that later. Now she just had to work like crazy so she could reap those results soon. She had no other option.

And she'd get back to doing just that after her visit with the rescue. Wearing a broad grin, she sailed into the shelter, boxes held high over her head. "Lunch, anyone?"

Claudia looked up from the paperwork spread out over the counter. "Are you serious? I'm always ready for Tony's pizza! What kind do you have?"

"Garbage Pies."

The older woman winked. "Um-*yum!* I should've worn sweats instead of jeans today. Garbage Pies are my faves, but they definitely call for a stretchy waist."

"No worries." Gabi winked. "I made these with no calories."

"I wish!"

They laughed, and then Gabi asked, "Where do you want me to put them?"

"You can take them to the staff room at the back of the utility side—"

"Or you can hand them over and I'll take the very best possible care of them," Zach said, an exaggerated look of mischief on his handsome, tanned features.

"Oh, no you don't." Claudia bounced down off the tall stool behind the counter and grabbed the boxes from Gabi. "I have to make sure poor Oscar's not stiffed out of his fair share of the pies. Remember, sharing's a good thing."

"Yes, Mother," Zach countered. "Have your kids ever gotten away with anything?"

Claudia turned to bump the door open with her rear and waggled her eyebrows at Zach. "Sure, they have, but not a whole lot. The other day I grounded Mark, and he complained about the unfairness of it all. Says he can't ever do anything, since any time he tries to break a family rule, I find out. He objects to my 'spies' all around town."

"That's good, when you have a sixteen-year-old guy in the house," Zach said.

As she followed them to the staff room, Gabi admired their easy relationship. The two of them bantered the whole way back, and Oscar joined them when he walked in from where he'd been hosing down the outside kennels. It made her think about her own friendships. She had two friends with whom she felt that comfortable. Ryder here in Lyndon Point was one, and Allie back in Cleveland the other.

Even though she hadn't planned on eating with Zach and the others, the dynamics between the shelter staff intrigued her, so she stayed when they invited her. Oscar, kind and polite and sweet as could be, was someone Gabi had loved ever since he'd started giving her cherry lollipops when she was all of three.

"I have a question for you, Oscar," she ventured after they'd made a huge dent in the pies. "Have you been to see Papa since his stroke?"

"Didn't hear he'd had one," he said, surprised. "I haven't done as much socializing these past few years. I'm so sorry about that, Gabi. Is he up to having visitors?"

"He'd love to see you, I'm sure. Give Mama a call, and see when would be a good time for them both."

"Too bad he'll miss the Adoption Fair," Claudia

added. "It's shaping up to be a whole lot of fun, and I'm sure he'd enjoy it."

Gabi nodded, but then something occurred to her. "If the weather's nice, there's no reason he has to miss it. It would probably do him good to get out of the house. Let's see what I can do. Mama would love to have a break, too."

"You're planning to be there, aren't you?" Zach asked.

"I wouldn't miss it for the world."

He tipped his head to the side, his gaze fixed on her. Just as his silent scrutiny began to make her blush, he seemed to come to a decision. "How's this sound? Since you're already here every day as it is, and since you like dogs and are planning to bring your dad to the event anyway, why don't you just join our volunteer staff? We're the only three regular employees, and Oscar's a volunteer because he won't let me pay him, but we couldn't run the place without our volunteers."

"It never crossed my mind. You do remember I don't live in town anymore, right?"

He frowned. "Can't forget it, since you say something about it every time we talk. But what's wrong with volunteering while you're in Lyndon Point? You'd have lots of time to spend with Houdini— your stray."

"Houdini's a great name for the great escape artist." Her thoughts whirled at Zach's other suggestion. "About the volunteer thing…it's not really a bad idea."

"C'mon, Gabi. Say yes," Claudia urged. "We'd have a great time together here. It's not like any other job I've ever had."

As the minutes went by, Gabi felt her objections melt away. Even the reasonable ones, like her lack of time or her unwillingness to grow a whole lot more attached to the terrier or, maybe more important, her reluctance to get any more involved with Zach than she already was.

"I'll think about it—"

"Aw, Gabi," Oscar said, teasing her as he had since she was little. "Agree. You know you want to."

She rolled her eyes and gave the older man a sheepish grin. "Well, I suppose."

"So you'll join our crew?" Zach asked, clearly expecting a positive response.

Gabi closed her eyes for a moment, sent up a silent plea for God to protect her from the potential heartbreak and then nodded. "It does sound fun. I'll join your volunteer crew. What do I have to do to become official?"

"Just sign an application," he said. "We'll call this meeting your formal interview."

"Really?" She laughed. "This is the weirdest interview ever."

Claudia cocked a finger toward Gabi. "See? I told you it was like no other job I ever had." She stood, crossed to the sink next to the small refrigerator against the wall to their right and pumped a squirt of antibacterial soap onto her hands. "Only thing wrong with Garbage Pies is how messy they are."

"Ah…" Gabi said, standing as well. "They're messy, but good."

"As pizza should be," Oscar added.

"As all good things in life generally are," Zach said.

Gabi grinned and waited her turn at the sink. When she'd dried her hands and tossed the damp paper towel in the trash can, she turned to head to the kennels for a short visit with Houdini. Only then did she realize Oscar and Claudia had already left the staff room. She and Zach were alone, and he stood close, very close, studying her again.

"I'm glad you agreed," he said, holding out a hand. "Welcome to the shelter—officially."

She placed her palm against his. "Me, too…"

At the contact, she let her words die off. Between the warmth in Zach's gaze and the gentle heat in his hand, she found her thinking short-circuited, and even breathing became a challenge.

She met his gaze, only to read admiration or appreciation—something dangerous—there. Oh, my! She was in real trouble now.

He'd argued nonstop with himself ever since lunch. Why on earth had he asked Gabi to volunteer at the shelter? He couldn't afford to get involved with anyone, not with everything he had on his plate right now. And Gabi was the last person he should ever get involved with, at any time. Her every other sentence was all about returning to Cleveland as soon as she helped her parents get back on their feet after her father's stroke. Even if he had the time for a relationship, a woman anxious to head halfway across the country as soon as possible wasn't the one for him.

Even if he couldn't keep his gaze away from her, couldn't stop smiling when she was around, couldn't keep from inviting her to hang around even more.

Not smart.

He turned off the clippers and hung them back from an S-hook in the pegboard on the wall. He returned to the new intake, and she rewarded him with a soft sniff of the hand and a timid lick. "I'm so sorry," he murmured as he picked her up and carried her toward the sink. "I know you're not going to like this, but I need to wash off those sore spots. Then I need to put medicine on them."

At least Houdini was thriving these days. The terrier had been given a complete veterinarian exam, which he passed without a single issue. He was ready for his forever home. But Zach felt it would be wrong for the dog to wind up with anyone other than Gabi.

Cleveland notwithstanding.

* * *

"I can't begin to tell you how hard they work at the shelter, and how happy they are doing it," Gabi told Allie later that night. "I wish it was that way at Executive Placements. I mean, I do enjoy my job, but it's not the same thing."

Allie stayed silent, and for a moment Gabi wondered if their call had dropped. Then, as she was about to hang up to dial again, her best friend responded.

"I'm going to be honest here," Allie said, strangely hesitant. "I've always wondered if you continue to work there because you think you have something to prove. Let's face it—you run the place, and make a bucket of money doing it, but you could do better just about anywhere else where they need an ace business major with experience." She cleared her throat. "So tell me the truth, do you work there because the work is really fulfilling?"

"How can you even ask me that?" she retorted. "I get the greatest satisfaction placing someone in the right job. Do you know how tough the market is out there? And these are families I deal with, not just job titles. Many of my clients are determined to provide for their wives and kids or to help their husbands with the family income."

"I get that. There's nothing wrong with what you do, but I'm not sure it's what *you* should be doing. Something about it has never seemed to fit you just right. Maybe you should be taking this time away to think about your future, about the direction where God would have you take the rest of your life."

The thought of brainstorming her future was intriguing, but the memory of her past battles for independence was stronger. "I'm perfectly satisfied with my job. All I want is to get back to it, and I'm certain it's where God wants me."

Again, Allie let the silence draw out. Gabi grew itchy from the tension. "Really, Al," she added, "I'm sure. I prayed and prayed about my job way back when I was looking, and Executive Placements was the answer. It ticked all my boxes for the perfect job."

"Time passes, Gabi, and God puts different things before you in different seasons."

"Sure. This is still my Executive Placements season."

"I still want you to pray about this. It matters."

Uncomfortable with the conversation and especially Allie's challenge, Gabi said a quick goodbye and hung up. What did her best friend expect her to do? Job hunting across multiple state lines was always a tough endeavor, as many of her clients learned whenever they wanted to move closer to family or to a particular part of the country. It didn't often work out the way they wanted, mainly because they weren't in place to make interview appointments as readily as local applicants. So, logistically, she couldn't do anything about a new job until she got back to Cleveland. Besides, she liked what she was doing.

It was Damon that drove her nuts.

He'd already called twice to ask when she planned to return to the office, even though she'd emailed him her work on the client files. She'd had to remind him she still had plenty of vacation time left— at least another four weeks, since she'd only taken a minimal amount of time off in the years she'd worked for him. Then, too, she had the right to family leave, if it came to that.

She just hated to have to remind him of this over and over again.

To be honest, it didn't help that she'd spent so much of her time at the animal shelter. It had only served to highlight obvious differences she wasn't sure she wanted to see. Zach was a far different kind of boss than Damon. She was looking forward to her volunteer stint. Even though she knew she shouldn't dwell on it, she couldn't stop herself from anticipating the time she would spend with Zach in the coming days. Her heart even seemed to kick up a tiny hitch every time she gave it a thought.

She was in trouble, but she couldn't dredge up the urge to do much about it. At least, not right then. Maybe later, when she was headed back to Cleveland. She had to wonder if that might not be too late.

Gabi learned soon enough the next day, right after

she showed up to visit the pup, what Zach and Claudia had in mind for her. Before more than a five-minute playtime with Houdini had gone by, Claudia came to look for her. "Good!" the older woman said. "I was hoping you hadn't left yet. Zach wants to see you in his office."

There it was! Gabi's middle did a flip of anticipation. At war with herself, she still made sure common sense won out. She reminded herself of her life back east. "Do you know what about?"

Claudia shrugged. "Must be about the fair, since that's all he's worked on this morning. He's never happy doing paperwork and admin stuff. He'd rather spend his time with the dogs and cats, and the adoptive families, so he's probably looking to delegate."

"I've noticed how much he loves the animals." Gabi remembered the times she'd seen him on the floor of the glass-walled room with a dog or cat on one side and a preschooler on the other, mom and dad looking on, protective anxiety on their adult faces. "I'll go find out what he's up to. See you later."

On her way down the kennel aisle, she realized the shelter was at full capacity. The fair couldn't come at a better time. She hoped many of the rescues would find families that day. Including Houdini. Even if her heart was in for a whole lot of hurt once he did.

To distract herself from that difficult eventuality,

she hurried along, knocked on the office door and cracked it open. "I heard you wanted to see me."

He waved her in. "The posters are ready for the businesses in town that agreed to display them for us. Since you're going back to Tony's, I was hoping you could deliver them."

"Sure, that's easy enough. Just tell me who gets one." Spurred by her work background, she decided to make a bold comment, one a volunteer might not be in the best position to make. "Since you suggested I volunteer, and I know how hard the three of you work all the time, I have to wonder if what you really need is to hire additional help, maybe part-timers."

He gave her a wry grin. "That would be a dream come true. Reality, on the other hand, says we're already stretching every penny we get so thin we hardly ever see a hint of the copper."

She'd suspected as much. "Now that you mention it, how is the shelter funded?"

"Lyndon Point has it in the budget."

"So you work for the town."

"Yes, I'm a government worker in that regard."

"What about donations?"

"Sure. I love to get them, but have you looked at the economy lately? Who has spare buckets of cash lying around, ready to spend on us?"

She sighed. "I know what you mean. I've been looking through Tony's books—well, the mountain of receipts my parents like to keep in shoe boxes. It doesn't paint a pretty picture."

"So what are *they* doing about it?"

"Absolutely nothing." When he frowned, she went on. "But I'm not about to sit on the sidelines, watching them go under because of the country's tough times. I'm making changes, tweaking things here and there, to put them on more solid footing."

"Really? Like what?"

Aside from that barest of suggestions to Mama last week, Gabi hadn't told anyone about her plans. Not even Allie. Maybe it was time to put her ideas into words, to hear herself describe what she'd done so far and what she still had to do.

She sucked in a deep breath before she met his silvery-gray gaze. "I want to turn Tony's into an up-scale bistro, a classier eatery—you know. That'll let us take advantage of the potential pool of customers from Seattle. You know how many come out to the coast on weekends and such. Puget Sound's the perfect draw. We can offer them a good place to spend their money and a great meal while they're doing it."

Twin lines appeared between his eyebrows. "A bistro?"

"A ritzy Italian eatery of some kind. I just know that Cleveland's got a bunch of trendy bistro-type places that are booming. It's the kind of place where people want to go."

A skeptical arch raised one of those expressive

eyebrows. "In this economy? I would think they'd be happier with a lower-budget pizzeria. I'd also think one that's well established and with steady patrons to talk it up to those visitors would make a better business model for your parents."

"The name we'd keep—maybe tweak it up to Antonio's. But there's no question the menu needs revamping. Mama has some unbelievably good family recipes that, fancied up for the foodie crowd, would be a hit."

"You're not planning to put your mother back to work, are you?"

"On the contrary. I've placed ads for an executive chef and a restaurant manager. I'll be interviewing the first one who responded on Monday morning."

To her surprise, he looked pained. "An executive chef and a restaurant manager might not be the best idea for you, and they don't come cheap."

She chose to ignore the first part of his comment. "I realize the costs involved, and I have enough to invest. I did my homework. Besides, job placement's what I do in my real life. It's my business to know what specific positions command."

"A headhunter...never would have pegged you for one."

She rolled her eyes. "I'd much rather you called me an executive placement specialist. I help clients forward their careers, not just find a new job."

For the most part. Gabi hoped the tiny stretch of

her job description didn't strike God as a lie, since it really wasn't. Not really.

She did help clients take their careers to the next level, but she also helped others find a job, any job. In this tough economy, many who had children in need of food, housing and health insurance counted themselves blessed just to earn a paycheck, no matter whether the work they did matched their skill set or not. It was all a part of what she did.

Zach clamped his lips together and shook his head. "Can't say this makes a whole lot of sense to me. Tony's is fantastic the way it is, and I wouldn't change a thing about it. Look at all your steady customers, and don't forget the part-time jobs your parents provide for the kids in town. There are even fewer jobs for them lately than for adults. Teens need work if they're going to further the funding for the education they'll need to provide for themselves in the future."

She raised one shoulder. "We can train them to work in a more upscale environment."

"Teens aren't usually the best servers in upscale establishments. They do best with serving the food they eat in a place they already know and love."

She ground her teeth as his words hit home. She hadn't thought of it in those terms before, but she had to make her choices, and her criteria were sound. "If that's the case, I'll be forced to hire older servers. I have to think of my parents' situation before I can take those kids' welfare into account."

"A great employer always thinks of his or her workers."

She'd seen him interact with Claudia and Oscar, and she knew he lived by that standard. But her position was different than his. Her plan wasn't based on the standards of Business Management 101's best practices. Papa's medical care had to come first—and saving Tony's was crucial to her parents' financial future. She held out her hands in helpless acceptance of the situation. "I hear what you're saying, Zach, but if the pizzeria goes under, then *no one* will have a job. Which means my parents won't be able to pay for Papa's care, and the town won't have another business to contribute to the local economy."

He straightened. "Go under? It's that bad?"

"Not yet, but bad enough that something has to be done before it reaches that point."

"That's too bad," he said, his features set in a tight line. "Just make sure you think this through carefully. It's not the kind of thing you can then go back and undo once it's done, no matter how much you might want to. I'd hate for you to go through something like that, especially since it never is easy to recover once it happens. It's all about the unintended consequences of your actions."

Gabi knew more lay behind his objection, but

from his closed expression she also knew he wasn't about to say any more. The time to go had arrived.

She picked up the stack of posters Zach had indicated earlier and turned to his office door, unwilling to face the disapproval in his gaze anymore. "I'll make sure these get to their new homes, and post ours at the checkout where customers can't miss it. I've even told our kids to talk up the fair as soon as they greet the customers at their tables."

"Thanks. I appreciate your help."

Okeydoke. That sounded like a definite goodbye. Maybe she'd misread the warm admiration she'd thought she'd seen in his expression the day before. Sure looked like it was a good thing she was leaving Lyndon Point soon, after all.

As she walked out, she heard a solitary sharp yap out in the kennel. It cut straight to her heart.

She made herself think of what would be best for the pup. Houdini *had* to find his forever family at the fair. Her sanity needed it. She had to put distance between her and Zach Davenport—and soon.

Once Houdini was adopted, she'd make sure she could perform her volunteer duties without having to see the shelter director every time she came in. She'd have to figure it out. One way or another.

Starting tomorrow.

Chapter Six

The "chef" Gabi interviewed Monday morning had little more to his résumé than fast-food grill work. He was a far cry from the gourmet cook she needed, and she hadn't had even a nibble on the restaurant manager opening. She had to do better—fast.

Just about all the month's accounts payable had come in, and Gabi knew she was about to wipe out the bank account when she wrote the necessary checks. Where was she going to find a suitable chef? And for a salary she could cover? Well, cover with her savings and the increased profits she hoped the bistro would soon bring in, of course.

"Gabriella!" her mother wailed, slamming the front door and running toward the kitchen where Gabi was buried under the blizzard of bills. "Look!" Mama shook a sheet of paper and a torn envelope almost against Gabi's nose. "*Cosa posso fare ora?* Huh? What am I going to do now?"

"Okay, okay, Mama. Calm down." She pulled out a chair and helped her mother to it. "Sit here for a moment, and let me get you a cup of coffee. Then I'll take a look at that."

"No!" Mama cried as Gabi grabbed a still-hot clean mug from the dishwasher. "You sit, too, Gabriella, and look at this. It…it's an outrage."

"That bad, huh?" She frowned as she set the full mug in front of her mother. "Okay, let me take a look at it."

Back in front of the mountain of bills, she spread out the piece of mail and scanned it. A moment later, she caught her breath. No wonder Mama was close to hyperventilating. It was the insurance company's explanation of benefits for Papa's hospital stay, and the total at the bottom of the list of charges was truly conniption-inducing.

Before she, too, lost it, she made herself take a couple of slow, deep breaths. "It's not what you think it is, Mama. It's not a bill, not one for us. It's an explanation of the charges from the hospital, but it's what was submitted to the insurance company, and this is the list for us to see those costs."

"Okay," her mother said after gulping down another shot of coffee, "but we have still co-pays and co-bills and co-whatever. We pay those, not insurance. I know that much, Gabriella."

"Of course there are co-pays, and we'll take care of those after the insurance pays out its part. Don't get upset before you have to. Besides, the hospital will let us set up a payment plan to make it easier to pay off our part of Papa's bill."

While her mother was no longer on the verge of passing out, she didn't look particularly comforted by Gabi's explanation. It was not a very good one, true, but it was broadly accurate.

The explanation of benefits did state their co-pay. And it was staggering. Not as enormous as the pre-insurance sum, of course, but still hefty. Especially in view of the paltry amount Tony's would make that month after they'd paid the regular bills due. Gabi wasn't sure how she was going to juggle it all.

At least, not before she got the new Antonio's up and running and making more money. Time had come to focus on that, instead of playing with a stray dog or mooning over the town's enigmatic animal shelter director. She had more important things to do.

But keeping to her latest decision proved harder to do than she would have imagined. She had offered to help at the shelter—and Claudia felt compelled to remind Gabi of her status as official volunteer every time they needed an extra hand getting the dogs ready for the fair.

That was how Gabi found herself hurrying to the shelter the Friday evening before the fair. Besides, she couldn't deny her enthusiasm to see Houdini again.

And Zach.

"I'm here, Claudia," she called out as she opened the shelter's heavy glass door. The five brass bells attached to the leather strap jangled long after the door had closed in her wake. "What's so important that you called me over right away?"

"We have twenty-four dogs that need baths for showtime tomorrow. We've even set up the sink in the bathroom to bathe the smaller ones. Please put on one of the rubberized aprons hanging in the utility section, and grab a little dog. I already set out a bottle of shampoo on the sink for you."

Uh-oh. "Are you sure you want me to do this? I've never bathed a dog before. Not even a human baby."

Claudia laughed. "Trust me, dogs are easier than humans. Take one of the kibble measuring cups, and use it to pour water over the dog. Then all you have to do is pump a little shampoo into your hand, scrub it all over, and pour more water to rinse. Just make sure you rinse the animals well. It's not good for their skin to leave shampoo residue behind. And don't get water in their ears."

Huh? "I'm not so sure about this, especially those parts about water in the ears or residue on the skin. I can give it my best shot, but I can't promise anything."

"You'll do fine." Zach walked up, cradling a six-month-old shepherd-mix puppy in his muscular arms. "By the way, hi, and thanks for pitching in on a Friday evening."

To her dismay, Gabi's heart kicked up its pace. She'd avoided him since the other day when he'd argued against her plans for Tony's—Antonio's—and now here she was responding to him just as she had from the very first time she'd seen him.

"We better hope I don't mess up," she said. "And I appreciate the break from mozzarella, tomatoes and anchovies."

He scrunched up his nose. "I can appreciate a lifelong vacation from anchovies."

"Philistine! You don't know what you're missing." Gabi grinned impishly up at him. "Now, I thought Claudia said I was to bathe the little guys. Are you taking care of that one you're holding, or am I taking over for you?"

"Neither. I brought him over for you, but I'm going to give you a couple of pointers, since I heard you say you've never given a dog a bath."

They walked into the staff bathroom together, and Gabi noticed not only a giant bottle of dog shampoo, but also a glass jar half-full of cotton balls. Since the items were perched on the top of the toilet water tank, she suspected they were there for the bathing session.

"What are those for?" she asked, as Zach began to fill the sink.

He glanced in the direction she indicated. "Those are to help keep water out of the dogs' ears. If it gets in there, they can develop ear infections, and we want to keep those from happening."

"Ouch! I went through a bunch of ear infections growing up, and I wouldn't want these poor things to get them, too. Show me what to do."

The next few minutes passed in companionable cooperation. After Zach made sure the water was at a good temperature for the puppy, he showed Gabi how to twist the cotton ball into a cone shape, and then demonstrated how to insert it into the dog's ear. Finally, he showed her how to use a washcloth on the dog's head to keep its exposure to the water down to a minimum.

"Now you're good to go," he said.

Dread tightened her middle. "I'm not sure about that."

He crossed his arms and leaned back against the doorjamb. "Hmm…where did the I-can-conquer-all Gabi I've been coming to know take off to? You know the one I'm talking about—the one who's on a mission to solve all her parents' business problems."

She stiffened. "Are you mocking me?"

"No." He straightened and moved toward her again. "Sorry if I came off that way. On the contrary, I'm surprised you feel so uncertain about something as simple as bathing a dog, when turning your parents' restaurant upside down doesn't seem to faze you one bit."

"Oh, trust me. I'm totally fazed, but I don't see

any other way to help them get through their current situation."

He waited for her to go on, but what was there for her to say? That her parents were being squeezed from every angle? Everyone else was, too. And the hospital bill? Everyone knew Papa had been ill, and everyone expected them to have to pay for the excellent care he'd received.

When she didn't speak further, he stepped closer still. "Something's wrong. Why don't you tell me about it? I've been told I'm a good listener."

The gentle kiss of his breath against her cheek both warmed her and sent chills through her. His nearness seemed to draw her like a toddler to a firefly, and her ability to think appeared to have vanished on a pure flight of fancy.

She drew a wispy, shuddery breath of her own. What was it about this man? No one else had affected her this way before.

And then she heard a sharp sneeze.

Zach laughed just a tiny bit away from her ear.

A tremor ran through her.

But before she could lose herself again in Zach's presence, the dog she was to bathe sneezed once more, then barked. Gabi shook herself free from the haze that felt as though Zach had wrapped around her.

She dunked the washcloth he'd given her in the warm water and gave the shampoo bottle pump a push. She then began to rub the little guy's head between the ears with her gentlest touch. "There's not much to tell. I have that mess with my parents' finances on my mind, and some days it weighs me down more than others. Not to mention the scare we had with Papa's health to begin with. I just need a little extra time with God tonight…and then I'll be okay."

"Okay. So what exactly weighed you down today?"

She shot him an exasperated look over her shoulder. "Persistent, aren't you?"

"A man doesn't get anywhere without persistence."

"You sure it's not plain old curiosity and stubbornness?"

He shrugged. "Does it matter what you call it? It's important not to quit. God's Word's pretty clear about that."

A believer. Good thing.

Her family's situation? Not such a good thing. "It's nothing different from what I just told you. We got a copy of the itemized statement the hospital sent to the insurance company. Mama saw it and went ballistic over the sums she saw. I can't say I blame her. I took a look at the bottom line, and it's overwhelming."

"I'm sure. He did have a stroke."

"That he did. And he had state-of-the-art medical care. I know it costs plenty, but when it's in black-and-white in front of you, it's a different thing. Maybe now you can see why I'm so determined to increase the profits at Tony's. I have to come up with that cash somehow."

"I'm sure the hospital will give you time to pay. That's what happened when my parents both died a short time apart. Their separate medical bills wouldn't have been too bad on their own, but when you added them together, they came with a whole lot of sticker shock."

She nodded as she poured a cupful of warm water over the puppy's back. "How many years did it take you to pay it all off?"

"I didn't count, and these days I make a point not to remember. I set up the account with the hospital's billing department, and they took care of automatically deducting a regular sum from my checking account every month. I celebrated when they notified me of their last withdrawal by buying a new set of bookshelves for all my coo—er, my books."

She didn't miss his bitten-off word, even though she hadn't caught enough to figure out what he'd been about to say. That was too bad. She didn't know much about him, and here she'd turned herself practically inside out revealing everything about herself and her family.

"Thanks for telling me about that," she said. "I appreciate your effort to lift my spirits."

Pain flashed through his expression but disappeared just as fast as it showed up. "I do know how tough life can be sometimes, especially when it comes to parents. And you're in a rough spot right now. I wish I could help—"

She waited for him to finish what he'd been about to say, but he didn't go on. When she glanced his way again, he just shook his head, then shrugged.

"It was nothing," he said. "Just forget it."

She supposed she'd have no other alternative, even though curiosity burned in her, and she suspected it hadn't been "nothing" but rather something important. Something that did matter.

"You do realize you're going to have to tell me a little about yourself, right?" She made sure her voice came out light and easy. "You know all there is to know about me by now. It's only fair for you to return the favor."

"There's not much to tell. I grew up in California, fell in love with animals, and when I saw the posting for this job opening here, I applied."

Gabi reached for one of the soft, fluffy towels stacked on the toilet seat cover to wrap her shivering charge. "There are tons of vast gaps in that sorry excuse for a life story, but I'll let you get away with it." She held the terry-cloth-wrapped pooch out toward him. "For now."

As she handed off the pup, their hands touched, and in spite of the slippery water on hers, they stood there, the contact unbroken. Once again, with Zach that close, Gabi felt the giddy rush of emotion she hadn't experienced before she'd met him. The light in his gaze seemed to echo what she felt, and his touch against her fingers brought her the oddest sense of mutual attraction, of loneliness dispelled, of welcome, of coming ho—

She gasped when she realized where her thoughts had strayed. She couldn't go there. She just couldn't. This wasn't home, and this man was all wrong for her.

Wrong, wrong, wrong.

She had to get away. Now. No matter how many stinky dogs she left behind. As she'd thought a number of times before, her sanity depended on it. No matter what she felt whenever she was in Zach's presence.

"I have to go," she mumbled as the alarm intensified inside her. "Now. Right now. Sorry."

She wrested her hands from beneath his and, with little more than a glance at his bewildered expression, she spun around and rushed out into the hall.

"But—"

"I'm sorry, so sorry. But, no, I have to go."

As the panic within pushed a prickling sensation up to her eyes, Gabi ran down the hall and into the reception room. She yelled a fast goodbye to Claudia then burst out onto the sidewalk. She didn't stop but kept on going in the direction of Tony's, tears welling in her eyes. *Oh, great.*

Guilt filled her. They needed her help. They wouldn't have called her otherwise. But, she'd been right back there. She had to get away.

Coward!

"You better believe it," she choked out. Perspiration beaded on her forehead as she ran uphill in the warm evening air.

Better a coward than brokenhearted. One half of her wanted to run back in and apologize to Zach, take the puppy back from him and spend the evening helping. The other half wanted to board the next flight to Cleveland and never set foot in Lyndon Point again. The place posed nothing but trouble for her.

As if she'd needed any more trouble here. Gabi had always felt like an outsider in the midst of her widespread family, since she couldn't relate to their aggressive togetherness and excessive pride in their heritage. At the same time, the kids in school wasted no opportunity to remind her of her status as an outsider. They'd repeatedly taunted her with those very same things her family held so dear.

She'd never been able to forget the time when Papa had come to school for a Career Day presentation. He'd spoken about running a restaurant, the challenges and rewards involved in the grueling work. While her classmates had sat in appropriate decorum and listened with suitable respect, once they'd all returned after lunch period, a group of the boys had drawn a twice-life-sized picture of herself, with a pizza for her face, lasagna for her limbs and squiggly spaghetti for hair. They'd then proceeded to regale her with their taunting version of the despised Dean Martin song.

Gabi shuddered.

As if that hadn't been humiliation enough, her *zia* Carlotta had joined forces with Mama and two older *cugini* and paid a visit to the principal. To this day, she had no idea what was said during that meeting, but knowing her aunt, mother and cousins, she had no doubt it had been blunt and to the point. The one thing she did know was that the kids in class had seriously resented her after that and made her life even more intolerable during her school years, pointing at her and whispering about "Gabi's Mafia."

Even now, when she saw some of them around town, they'd remind her of their pranks and laugh.

No, Lyndon Point was not for her. For many reasons.

And now there was Zach.

She had to keep reminding herself, a recent—and happy—Cleveland transplant, that he was content to build a life for himself in Lyndon Point. That, right there, made him wrong for her. Without a doubt.

But why, then, did his presence at her side, his friendship and his touch feel so right?

* * *

The next day, Zach was still trying to figure out what he'd done to chase Gabi out of the shelter as though he'd set a feral feline on her trail. For the briefest of moments there, when they'd both held the wet puppy between them, his hands over hers, he'd felt a powerful connection between them. He was sure she'd felt it, too.

Then she'd pulled that disappearing act. He had to wonder if he'd mistaken the attraction he'd sensed between them. He'd thought it was mutual. Now, however, he'd begun to suspect he was more likely unappealing to her.

Either that or his curiosity had come across in a negative way. But he thought she'd been okay with his questions. In fact, she'd begun to ask him questions of her own.

Not that he'd been prepared to answer any of them, since his defeat in Sacramento still loomed too raw in his heart. In spite of last night, however, he suspected she was about the only person to whom he could imagine revealing all about that disaster—when he reached the point where he could talk about it at all.

That made her flight hurt even more.

He hated to admit it, even just to himself, because he hadn't thought he'd invested much emotion in their *acquaintance,* since he really couldn't call it a relationship. At least, he hadn't done so yet. But he had thought there was potential there. At this point, he could only call himself a fool. And she was supposed to show up any minute now at the main booth set up outside the shelter. Gabi had agreed to help Claudia with the adoption paperwork, but she'd said that on Thursday, before he'd scared her away.

He wondered if she'd even show up.

"Hey, boss!" Claudia called out. "Where did you put the box of leashes?"

"Do you mean the ones with the shelter's phone number printed on them?"

"Yep. The multicolored ones we planned to give out with each forever family placement."

Hmm…he'd been so preoccupied with what had happened the evening before, all he could remember was picking up the box in the utility section of the building. What he'd done with it after that was beyond him. He looked around with a sinking sense of helplessness. "I'm sorry. I can't remember."

Claudia rolled her eyes. "Too much on your mind, huh?"

"I guess."

"Or should I say *someone's* too much on your mind?"

Zach felt his cheeks heat up, but he didn't want to own up to what he'd been thinking. Or feeling. Especially not to Claudia. "What do you mean?"

"C'mon, boss. I'm not stupid. Besides, I'm the one who was at the counter when Gabi did her personal rendition of the 'Flight of the Bumblebee' sans music last night. What happened? What did you do to her?"

"Me?" His voice rose with outrage. "Why would you think *I* did something to her?"

"Well, since she didn't drop a wet dog, dump a full bottle of shampoo on the floor or kick over a new bag of kibble, and she left less than a half hour after she came, leaving us with all the guests to bathe on our own, I figure you must have had something to do with it."

"All I did was reach out for the wet dog! How could that upset her?"

Claudia opened a box of pens and poured them into the plastic basket she'd set next to the stack of adoption applications. "Are you sure that's *all* you did?"

"Of course I'm sure. I was there, wasn't I?"

"Maybe it was something you said rather than what you did, then."

He ran a hand through his hair. "I didn't say anything offensive or controversial. We were talking about the pizza place, her parents, anchovies and ear infections. I don't see anything to chase a woman away in any of that."

Claudia's jaw dropped. "Really?" she said a moment later. "That's what you talked to a beautiful woman about? Oh, you're weird. No wonder she ran away."

"No way. We were doing fine while we were talking. Her vanishing act had to do with her giving me the dog. That was when she snapped." He shook his head. "I think it's…well, I think it's just me. I scared her off, but I don't really know how. Or why."

Claudia snorted. "That's definitely not it. I'm a woman, and I know the signs. She likes you a lot more than just fine."

Again, his cheeks blazed. "You couldn't prove it by her reaction yesterday."

"Hush!" Claudia said. "Here she comes now. I'm just thrilled she didn't decide to ditch the fair. I'm really counting on her help."

Zach's relief struck harder than he might have expected. He watched her approach, and an appreciative smile spread across his lips without him even thinking about it. She looked great, her hair up in the trademark ponytail. With the sun shining down, the thick waves looked darker and silkier than usual. Her lightly tanned skin glowed with vitality, and the pink knit top she wore that day enhanced the warm, golden tones. As she often did, she wore shorts that showed off the lines of her gently curved legs, but instead of another pair of her cutoff denims, these shorts were tailored khakis of walking length.

The sparkly pink sandals on her feet made him smile even more.

Zach didn't want to admit it, but just the sight of her did something to him in the vicinity of his heart.

And he suspected he was in deeper trouble here than he could have imagined when he'd first laid eyes on her the day she'd first showed up at the shelter.

In spite of that suspicion, he was glad she'd come. Really glad. And before he chased her away again, he had to make himself scarce. He didn't want another repeat of the night before. Certainly not before the fair was over. The dogs needed to be adopted. He'd figure out later what he'd done wrong.

And how to handle the unexpected attraction.

He hurried toward the shelter in search of the missing box of leashes, grateful for the distraction, even though he still couldn't stop thinking about Gabi.

"Lord?" he murmured. "If I did something wrong, if my questions offended her or pushed her too far, please show me. And give me the words to apologize. I want to make things right again."

Fortunately for him, the morning grew hectic in no time. He found the box of leashes right behind a commercial-sized tub of cat litter, and he rushed it outside. The next couple of hours passed by in the same kind of blur.

Unwilling to make matters any worse, he held himself back from the general excitement around the table where Gabi and Claudia took care of the potential adoptive families. The shelter's crew of fifteen volunteer foster parents took turns holding the leashed shelter residents, as well as those they'd taken into their homes, no more than ten feet away from the table. Kids of all ages swarmed the area, begging their parents for a pet.

When Zach brought out another one of the three shepherd-mix puppies who'd lost their mother to a hit-and-run, he noticed that Gabi's parents had joined her. He was glad to see them, especially when he caught sight of her father's smile.

Then Oscar came outside with Houdini in his arms. Zach winced. He'd hoped to keep that particular guest inside until the end of the fair, since he didn't want him adopted by anyone but Gabi. He still believed the two of them belonged together.

"Who do you have there now, Oscar?" Claudia asked, turning. As soon as she saw the dog in the older man's clasp, she swiveled back to look at Gabi.

Gabi glanced at Oscar, and Zach saw her blanch. No matter what she said, she wasn't ready for Houdini to go to a forever home that wasn't hers. Zach didn't know what to do next, and his brain wasn't engaging. All he could think about was the obvious pain in Gabi's gaze. And how he might ease it.

Out of the corner of his eye, he caught Gabi's father's delight when Houdini wriggled out of Oscar's arms and into his daughter's lap. That was when the idea struck Zach.

He gave the pup a few minutes to spend with her, enjoying the easy smile on her pretty face, and then, when Houdini began to settle down on her lap, he made his move.

"Mr. and Mrs. Carlini, I'm so glad you could come." He then turned to face the older man. "And I'm especially glad to see you recovering so well."

"Little by little," Gabi's father answered, clearly pleased by Zach's attention. "It's good to come, see the dogs."

Nodding genially at the portly, balding gentleman, Zach didn't miss the slowed speech but was glad to observe no other obvious impairment. Gabi had told him the wheelchair was due to general weakness from the stroke itself and the need for physical therapy to develop strength again. "Have you met our special pup yet?" he asked.

The owner of Tony's grinned. "All is special, no?"

"Ah, but I have one that's more special than the others." He sidled behind Gabi's chair. "Here. I'd like you to meet him."

In a fluid movement, he reached down and, to his surprise, Houdini hopped into his hands. As he walked over to Mr. Carlini, he didn't miss the glare Gabi sent his way. It made him wince, but since he was already in her bad graces, he figured it wouldn't do much more damage than had already been done.

"Can I set him on your lap?" he asked.

Gabi's father patted his thighs. "Here. I'm ready."

As soon as he lowered Houdini into place, the dog rose on his rear legs, placed his front paws on

Mr. Carlini's chest and then stretched to sniff the man's chin. Moments later, he yapped, licked his new friend and turned around in a couple of circles before he plopped down as though the lap was a soft, plush pillow. One he owned, of course.

"Antonio!" Mrs. Carlini cried, charmed. "He's so sweet!"

Gabi looked from the dog to her father to Zach and back to Houdini. He saw her struggle with her emotions, and he wondered if she felt as though the dog had abandoned her. Much like the unreasonable sensation he'd experienced the night before when she'd run away from him.

But then, after a couple of minutes ticked by, she glanced back up at him, a tentative smile on her lips. "Thanks. Looks like it was a good idea."

He shrugged, more pleased by her response than he should have been but unable to stop the feeling. Before he could do more than shrug, a new wave of people surrounded the table, and he turned to head back into the shelter building. Time to bring more homeless pets for inspection. And hopefully homes.

To his dismay, however, when he came back outside, he saw Gabi clasped in a tall man's tight embrace. An unpleasant jab of something close to jealousy zinged through him. But when they separated, he relaxed. It was the mayor, a happily married man, and, as Gabi had said, a distant relative.

Zach walked up to them, his hand held out to

Ryder Lyndon. "Glad to see you could make it," he said as they shook. "Maybe we can talk you and your wife into taking one of our charges home with you. Your little girl would love a puppy. Or maybe a kitten."

Ryder's eyes widened, and he darted glances in all directions, clearly looking for escape. Did that tendency run in the family? Gabi laughed. "I'm not sure it's the best of times for a new pet to join their family."

"Oh, there's never a bad time to adopt a friend."

"Ah…" The mayor was clearly flustered. "Hate to tell you, but there is. The worst time to get a new dog is when you have a toddler running around. The last thing we want is for him to terrorize a dog—or for the dog to knock him over."

Gabi's eyes twinkled merrily. "Or for the puppy to leave…*things,* shall we say, for him to discover."

Zach grimaced. "I get your point. I guess timing does matter sometimes. Even when it comes to pet adoption."

"Actually, I'm going to pass on a pet right now for the very best reason," the mayor said. "My wife would kill me if I brought a dog home. She has her hands full with our kids and with her store. She's starting a new series of quilting classes for the summer, and she's had to expand from two to three sessions, since the interest was much greater than she'd expected."

Zach chuckled. "As the outstanding government official that you are, I'm sure you can appreciate the business she's bringing to town."

Ryder rolled his eyes. "Have to wonder what you're going to hit me up for next."

Zach held his hands up in a gesture of surrender. "Not a thing, since a dog's out of the question. Just thinking of the future of this town, and all the good you're doing for it."

"Just as I'm appreciating this crowd you've drawn here today, then. I don't know half these people."

"Didn't I tell you Ryder would recognize a good thing when he saw it?" Claudia called out from where she handed a form to another family. "And Lyndon Point's Adoption Fair has turned out to be a huge success."

Zach glanced at Houdini, whose slender legs gave a twitch in his sleep. For selfish reasons, he hoped it wouldn't be *too* huge a success. He turned to Gabi and found their gazes catching, holding. Understanding flew between them. She didn't want Houdini adopted out any more than he did. Even though she'd insisted time after time it was the right thing to do, that it was what she wanted.

She didn't want to lose the terrier, after all.

Maybe she would change her mind about running away from him, too. Whatever that had been all about.

But Zach knew better than to push his luck.

Especially in public. In any event, he should go check in with his foster families. Hopefully, that wouldn't take too long and then he could come back and check on the table again.

Maybe he'd even ask Gabi to have lunch with him.

No pressure. They'd be eating with half the town.

It wouldn't be a date or anything. At least that's what he kept telling himself.

Chapter Seven

Gabi stole yet another glance at Houdini, who'd taken over Papa's lap as though he'd been doing it ever since the day he was born. Her father appeared just as happy with the situation as the dog. And while she loved the dog's apparent instant acceptance of Papa—and vice versa—she couldn't help feeling apprehensive.

Her father was charmed. So was Houdini. But neither Mama nor Papa was in any condition to take on a project as significant as dog ownership at the moment. They were especially unprepared for the headaches that came with housebreaking a young dog.

Her time in Lyndon Point would not last much longer, even if every time she looked at her parents, a brand-new twinge of anxiety would strike. It had all begun after she'd come to grips with their financial situation. But no matter what, she still had to get back to Cleveland soon. Damon's calls grew more insistent and his questions more pointed. The last thing she wanted was to wind up unemployed because of a dog. That would leave their family in yet another level of financial strain. Lack of income for her, in the current job market, could precipitate a move back to Lyndon Point if she couldn't find something suitable. What if—

No. She couldn't start to think that way, not yet. It was much better if she focused on Papa's enjoyment of the dog today. A lovable dog, for sure, but a dog they couldn't take home.

And then there was Zach and how attracted she was to him. For a final twist of tension, of course. She sighed. She lived a complicated life.

"It is true!" a woman squealed, cutting into Gabi's somber thoughts. "I'd heard you'd come home, but I didn't believe it. Now here you are."

Hannah McRoberts, a tad plumper than the last time Gabi had seen her high school classmate, stood in front of the table, her hand on a stroller bearing twin munchkins in identical green-and-white outfits.

"I don't have to ask what you've been up to, do I?" she asked, as she stepped out from behind the table and hugged her friend.

"Marriage and motherhood." Hannah's grin grew as wide as the Pacific Northwest blue sky overhead. "And a severe lack of sleep, too."

Gabi laughed. "I can see why. They're gorgeous! What are your little ones' names?"

"Jonathan and Jeremy, and they're four months old."

The two women spent a few minutes catching up with each other, and a short while later, Hannah left after she'd adopted a beautiful young silver-gray cat. They'd also agreed they needed a whole lot more time to fill in the blanks of the past few years than a chance encounter at a town event. They'd made plans to meet for lunch, and Gabi couldn't wait for the chance to get reacquainted again. It struck her in a weird way to recognize how much she'd missed of a good friend's life.

When Hannah was gone, a group of half a dozen kids lined up in front of the table where Gabi's friend had just stood. They asked reams of questions about pet adoption and oohed and aahed over the animals on display.

"Why don't you guys bring your mom or dad down here?" Gabi asked after a while. "We'd love to help you take a new best friend home today. But we can't do that without your parents. We need a grown-up to sign the paperwork."

Three of the kids scampered right off. The others stayed where the foster family volunteers had the leashed future adoptees on display. Even after the last two boys had left, a petite girl with dark hair in braided pigtails remained, clearly captivated by a multi-breed mix female rescue. Child and dog seemed well suited to each other, since both appeared gentle and quiet. Gabi wondered why she hadn't run off to bring back a parent, since she clearly wanted the dog.

"Where's your mom?" Gabi finally asked as she knelt next to the child and the dog.

She didn't look up but instead continued to pet the animal. "Working."

That set off an alarm. "You're here all alone? How soon does she get off work?"

"What time is it?"

Gabi noticed right away which of her questions went unanswered. How sad—and worrisome. "It's eleven o'clock."

A thin shoulder rose. "A few more hours. She works until three."

All that time unsupervised... The situation didn't sit well with Gabi. After all, this girl couldn't be more than nine or ten years old and shouldn't be wandering the Adoption Fair alone. "We'll still be here at that time, you know. Why don't you stay with us and play with the dogs until then? That is, if you'd like to do that."

During that time, she could make sure the child had food and drink and, most of all, adult supervision. "Then you can bring her down here when she's done working. We'll see if this dog you like so much is still available at that time. As soon as your mom signs the paperwork you can take your new pet home with you."

The little girl's eyes filled with tears. "She won't sign."

"Really?" Gabi reached out to scratch the dog behind the ears as the child stroked the animal's back. "What makes you so sure?"

"Mommy says we can't afford anything."

Great. She'd meant to encourage the girl, but she'd only managed to make her feel worse. "Why don't you bring your mom down to see us, anyway? I'm sure we can come up with some kind of arrangement for you."

"Really?" A glimmer of hope brightened the youngster's expression. "You think?"

She prayed she could. "I'll do everything I can to help," she promised. "Just make sure you come and look for me with your mom."

"Okay. I can do that."

"And please hang out with us until then. It'll be lots of fun for us to have you here."

As soon as the child sat and crossed her legs, the dog crawled into her lap, and they looked settled in for the duration. Not that Gabi expected a youngster that age to stay seated for that many hours, but at least the little girl seemed content to stay where Gabi could keep an eye on her.

"By the way," she called as she paused on her way back to her chair, "my name's Gabi. What's yours?"

"Emma."

"I'm so glad to meet you, Emma. I think we're going to be good friends."

At the table, she leaned close to Claudia. "Hey, change chairs with me, would you? I want to keep an eye on that little girl over there."

Claudia glanced across the way. "Oh, sure. Emma's mother is the nicest woman. She lost her husband a few months ago. He was military—navy, like my husband—but he died overseas."

Gabi nodded, remembering what Claudia had told her about her husband, a career officer at the nearby Everett navy base. Then Claudia continued, frowning.

"She's having trouble getting her benefits sorted out, and they're struggling at the moment. We all try to help out whenever we can."

"Would they be a good family to place a dog with?"

"They'd be great, but I doubt they can afford the adoption fee or the cost of food right now."

Gabi sent up another quick prayer and came to an even faster decision. "They can now. Make sure no one adopts the dog on her lap. When her mother comes, you can figure out how you want to tell her, but their fee is now paid, as well as a couple of big sacks of food. They'll have plenty, at least for the next few months."

Claudia's eyes opened wide. "Are you sure?"

"Positive."

Just then, Gabi felt a strong hand clasp her shoulder. "That's the nicest thing anyone's done around here in a while," Zach said. "We can help out with the food, as well. Not that we have funds to spare, but I know the shelter can share a bit of kibble here and there once your portion's gone."

Gabi glanced up and met his admiring gaze. A shiver of alarm sped through her, but the pleasure his admiration brought her squelched her more sensible side. "Thanks—"

"Gabriella!" Edna Lyndon cried. The sixty-something Realtor, a relative so distant Gabi didn't even know what the connection was, grinned from ear to ear as she plopped down her chic handbag on the table in front of Gabi. "I'm so glad you're here for your parents, dear heart. They've really needed your help."

Again, an unwanted touch of guilt zipped through Gabi. Instead of thinking about it, however, she thought only of the fun Edna always brought along with her. "I'm so happy to see you! What have you been up to?"

"Selling Lyndon Point, of course." She patted her ultrashort, slightly spiked silver hair, and her eyes sparkled with a healthy dose of humor. "I'm a mogul, didn't you know? Of the most modest, local sort, of course."

"Oh, I think you can give yourself a little more credit than that, Aunt Edna," Gabi said, hugging the older woman. "I hear you're doing wonders to help the town's property values."

Edna grew serious. "I love my hometown, and if doing something I enjoy and am good at can help it, then I'm all in. You might want to think about that, sweetie. We can use your talents around here. And your parents can use your company, and help, as you know."

"C'mon, Aunt Edna." Gabi blew out a frustrated breath. "You're the last person I expect that line from. You're the kind of businesswoman I've always looked up to. You have to understand I can't build a career here in this tiny town."

"Ha!" Edna smacked her fists on her generous, silk-clad hips. "Seattle's our very own backyard. You want to tell me there's no future for a top-notch career placement specialist in a major city of that size? Try again, kiddo."

"Yes, but—"

From a few feet over, Papa called out, "Don't waste spit, Edna. She no listen. *é molto ostinata,* is stubborn, my girl."

Edna chuckled and shook her head. Then she turned back to Gabi. "Seriously, my dear. You really should take the time to look around while you're here. This is where you belong. We're all here, your whole family. There's nothing for you to hare off to Ohio for. And no way, no how, to just find a job—excuse me, a *career.*"

"But—"

"Listen to me, Gabi. You should—"

"Okay, Aunt Edna," Gabi interrupted when the latest "should" came out. "What if we talk about this some other time? I'm working here, and don't have time to rehash my whole career plan while folks want to adopt pets." She sighed, trying hard to control her irritation. "So which one of these pooches do you want to take home with you?"

"Ha!" Edna exclaimed. "Goes to show just how long you've been gone. I don't think Archie and Edith would much appreciate if I brought a canine home to them."

Gabi wasn't sure she wanted to know but asked anyway. "Archie and Edith?"

"Yes, dear. The Bunkers." She chuckled, then went on. "I stopped by here when Zach first re-opened the shelter a few months ago, and adopted a pair of sassy felines. With all the crazy hours I keep, they're the perfect companions for me."

"Yes, but Archie and Edith Bunker? From that old TV show?"

"Of course. What else would you name the orneri-est tom and the most docile girl cat ever?"

"Good grief. That sounds like a self-fulfilling prophecy right there."

Edna grabbed her purse and hefted it onto her shoulder. "Come over and meet them. You'll see." She turned to Zach and held a check out to Claudia. "Just wanted to drop off a donation for the good work you're doing. Keep it up."

A chorus of thanks greeted the good-sized sum. One thing was certain: While Edna was a successful businesswoman, she didn't have a stingy hair on her spiky head. Everyone knew of her generosity. If only more of those who could follow in her footsteps did like her, then the shelter's finances wouldn't be quite so tight.

Then Edna faced Gabi as she started to leave.

She braced herself.

"Remember, dear heart," the older woman said. "You really should—"

"I'll think about it, and I'll talk to you later." At the skeptical rise of the silvery eyebrows, Gabi added, "I promise."

Edna's gray eyes narrowed. "I'll hold you to it. Now don't you try and sneak back off to Cleveland without talking to me, you understand?"

"I understand."

Edna marched off, and Gabi collapsed back into her chair, the start of a headache throbbing in her temple. "I'm sorry about that." She glanced from Claudia to Zach. "This wasn't the time or place for it."

"It's okay," Zach said, patting her shoulder. "Come on. Let's go grab some lunch. You've been here for hours, and anyone can tell that wasn't easy for you, no matter how terrific Edna is. How about we head over to Birdie's Nest for a bite? Unless you want pizza from the stand you set up over there."

Gabi glanced partway down the block where her crew was doing quite a bit of business with the lunch crowd. "You're kidding, right? More pizza?"

He grinned.

She pushed her chair back. "Nah. Much as I love the stuff, a plain old burger from the Nest will hit the spot a lot better."

"Let's go, then. Most people are taking time to eat right now, and I think Oscar can help Claudia for a while. When we get back, we'll take turns so everyone gets a chance to have lunch."

"Go ahead," Claudia urged. "Oscar's just walking out of the building, and all the fosters are here. If a mob suddenly descends on me, someone will lend a hand."

Gabi grinned. "When we get back, you might want to head home for a while. Mr. Mom might need a bit of rescuing by now."

Claudia rolled her eyes. "If I know my husband, he's got the kids lined up, doing drills like good little navy plebes. He drives me crazy sometimes with his neat, disciplined meticulousness—especially when it comes to the kids."

Gabi laughed, having heard Claudia's refrain before. "Maybe it's the kids that need the break by now, then."

The other woman joined in the laughter. "Okay,

point taken. I'll go home for a half hour after you two get back from lunch. Enjoy!"

A moment later, Gabi and Zach headed back up Sea Breeze Way toward Main, where Birdie's Nest was located. Everyone in Lyndon Point made a habit of eating at the town diner at least once a week, if not for the excellent homemade meals and desserts, then for the chance to catch up on all the local events.

Then she realized what she'd done. She'd agreed to eat with Zach Davenport. Not that there was anything wrong with it, but she'd run away from him the night before when she'd realized too much was developing between them. A broken heart wasn't the kind of souvenir she wanted to take back to Cleveland.

A sideways glance revealed an equally pensive Zach, his gaze fixed on the sidewalk, not unlike her. Could he feel the same way she did? She didn't think she'd misinterpreted those appreciative looks he'd sent her way, but would he really be foolish enough to consider a relationship with a woman who was about to return halfway across the country? Maybe she needed to discuss the matter with him.

At the thought, her stomach knotted and the root of the headache that had birthed in her temple earlier grew to a sudden pounding. That conversation was the last one she wanted to have. It would be even worse than dissecting her life with Aunt Edna.

"It's going well, don't you think?" Zach asked.

Grateful for the diversion from her thoughts, she gave him a weak smile. "Much better than I thought it might. Pets are a responsibility, and I suspect most people's lives are already overextended."

"That's one of the reasons we're so disciplined about our neutering program. We neuter the surrendered animals, and for those who are adopted before the vet's performed the procedure, we have the new owners agree to wait until it's done before they take their new pets home."

"It's not the animals that come through the shelter that are the problem, though."

"I know. We're doing all we can to spread awareness with public service announcements at all the civic organizations and social groups in town. We do presentations at all the schools, too."

"Have you seen any progress?"

He shrugged. "Some. I checked with the Lyndon Point Animal Hospital and the vets in nearby towns, and they have seen an increase in procedures, but I don't think it's been a drastic improvement."

"Small steps in the right direction always lead somewhere. The hardest thing is finding the patience to keep doing what you're doing."

A smile twitched at the corner of his lips. "That's true."

Fortunately for Gabi, who'd run out of pertinent and encouraging things to keep the conversation going, they'd arrived at Birdie's Nest. Zach opened the door for her and, as always, a wallop of nostalgia hit her when she stepped inside.

Cheerful chitchat hummed through the place, keeping pace with the fifties music playing overhead. Plates clattered in a kind of punctuation, and the scents of coffee, cinnamon-and-sugar-scented apple pies, Birdie's trademark savory meat loaf, her crispy fried chicken and the equally appealing French fries lured Gabi deeper down the crowded aisle. Birdie prided herself on the comfort and welcome she offered her patrons. Gabi knew the woman's approach was nothing but a huge success.

Until she walked in, however, she hadn't realized how much she'd missed the homey appeal of the place. And whenever she left town, she missed it more than she wanted to admit. The Nest was part of her life, one she still loved.

"Is this good?" Zach asked, indicating a booth at the back of the diner.

"Perfect. I'd much rather sit at the end here than near the door. There are always too many people coming in and out."

"It's a great place," he said after they'd sat. The teenage waitress handed them huge vinyl-covered menus immediately. "I don't know if I'd have survived my first couple of weeks in town without it," he added. "I didn't have any time to try to figure out what to feed myself after putting in sixteen-hour days at the shelter."

"Not much of a cook, then, are you?"

A strange expression crossed his face. "Uh…well, no. It's not that. More like too tired to come up with menus, go shopping for the right ingredients and then come home to prep and cook after all those hours of work."

"Really? Nuking a frozen meal's a breeze." She winked at him. "Ever hear of a microwave?"

He scoffed. "It's never the same thing. You need to cook fresh to have *food,* the real thing. Microwaves are just tools for thawing stuff you forgot to take out or to reheat leftovers."

"Ah, a total foodie."

"I don't consider myself one." He drew a deep breath, then let it out slowly. "But you could say that."

The waitress came up, pad at the ready. "What can I get you?"

Zach waved for Gabi to go ahead, clearly relieved at the interruption. How strange.

Still, Gabi dropped the subject and handed the girl the menu. "I'd like the third-pounder with everything on it, iced tea—no sugar, slice of lime—and for dessert, Birdie's apple pie with a ton of vanilla ice cream."

Zach let out a slow whistle. "You don't mess around, do you?"

"Not when it comes to food."

He smiled with appreciation. "I like that in a woman."

Gabi's cheeks heated up and she grasped for the first thing to say to diffuse the moment. "What do you expect? I was raised in a pizzeria. Food and my family go together in a big way."

He ordered the same, except for a root beer instead of the tea. "You could still be one of those women who eat a lettuce leaf and a pea, and then call it a meal."

She wrinkled her nose. "Nope, not me. Give me a burger, lasagna, chicken potpie—just about anything goes."

"How 'bout pizza?" he asked, his tongue firmly planted in one cheek.

"Only every other meal, for variety's sake!"

The lighthearted banter developed from there, Zach clearly as determined as she was to avoid conversational land mines. Before they left, Gabi ordered a child's burger meal.

"I'm glad you reached out to Emma," he said, cupping her elbow as they ambled down the front steps of the diner. "She's a sweet little girl. She comes into the shelter every so often while her mother goes grocery shopping. She loves dogs."

"I could see that. She melted my heart, and besides, we're kindred spirits. I couldn't just ignore her connection with that rescue—"

"That's Penelope Poo."

"Ew, what a lousy name. Who did that to her?"

He laughed. "That was Claudia's little girl. She insisted."

"Plain Penny's much nicer. I'll have to talk to Claudia about that child of hers. What is she teaching her?"

They made their way back to the shelter, their conversation still easy and comfortable. Gabi was glad. What might have turned into a disaster had instead been a wonderful time.

Back at the adoption table, Gabi turned to Zach. "Thanks. I really enjoyed the break."

"It was all my pleasure—and I mean that. It's a cliché, but it hits the mark this time."

She grinned but had nothing more to add without embarrassing herself again. She realized a number of eyes were focused on them. Fortunately, she had Emma's lunch in hand. "Go, go!" she told Claudia. "I have this to take care of, but I'm ready to substitute for you."

Although the older woman's expression promised future interrogations over the time spent with Zach, she didn't put up any argument and instead headed for home and the well-earned break. With a sigh of relief, Gabi turned toward the gaggle of dogs and foster families. She noted that Emma was still there.

"Hey," she said as she approached the child. She

was glad to see Emma had found another little girl to play with. "I hope you like hamburgers."

Emma turned around, her eyes wide with surprise. "That's for me?"

"I promised, didn't I?"

The smile came slowly but surely. "Thanks! I love burgers."

Satisfied with her efforts, Gabi walked away as Emma scrabbled in the bag for her meal. She couldn't wait to place the dog—Penny—with Emma and her mother, but the thought of Emma all alone while her mother worked on Saturdays still bothered her. She'd have to see what she could do about that.

"See, Gabriella?" her mother said. "You're good with little girl. You need husband and babies. Not to run to Cleveland. Bah!"

Gabi blushed but pretended not to have heard her mother by relieving Oscar from his table duties. She focused on the people who'd come to see the dogs and cats, and those who were interested in the low-cost spay-and-neuter program. She was glad Zach had told her about that, since she now knew she could point the families in the right direction.

After a half hour, however, she glanced toward her parents again, who'd been sitting under the shelter building's entrance overhang. Even though she'd made sure they had cold water and light refreshments the whole time, it had been a long morning for Papa. She excused herself from the volunteer who'd sat in Oscar's chair at her side and headed toward them.

Just then, Zach walked up, a bag of dog treats in hand. "Do you think your father would want to give Houdini his cookie?"

"Ask him, but I'm sure he'd love to."

As she expected, Papa made a production of giving the tasty bit to the dog, who, of course, begged for more.

"Hey!" Zach said, scratching behind the pup's lush ears. "You've really got a thing for food, don't you?"

"Always has," Gabi said. "Remember his Dumpster escapades?"

"Who could forget?"

Out of the corner of her eye, Gabi caught Papa's attempt to smother a yawn. "But now it's time for me to help Mama get Papa home." She turned to her father. "You've been out here a long time, and the doctor said you shouldn't wear yourself out."

"I'm okay. See? I have new friend with me."

"Yes, but you're recovering from a major health challenge. You need your rest." She gave him a fierce glare. "Come on. Don't argue, and hand over your friend."

She reached out to pick up Houdini, but to her surprise, the dog scurried closer to her father.

"That's unusual," Zach commented, watching. "He's always jumping to get close to you."

She nodded. "Maybe he can sense we're family."

Zach arched a brow. "That's stretching it. I think he's fickle, and has given his heart to your father."

"What's that word, that *fickle?*" Papa asked.

"It means that you change your mind very easily," Gabi said. "Let's try this again. I need to take him back to where the volunteers are. And you need a nap."

Papa nuzzled Houdini's neck. "Then *fickle* means I change my mind, too, Gabriella. I no go home now. I stay with…with…" A huge yawn overtook him.

"Aha!" Gabi crowed. "You see? It's time to go. Let me take Houdini back."

Again, she went to pick up the terrier, but this time, the dog gave her an impertinent look and argued back in his unique if garbled throaty language.

"Don't *you* give me a hard time, too, mister." She reached out once again, and he yapped his objection. "Aw, give me a break. Papa's got to head home. Come with me, buddy."

As though he'd understood every word she'd uttered, and still disagreed, Houdini turned three circles on her father's lap and curled up again, his tail wrapped in a neat C around his body.

"He told you," Zach said, between chortles.

"Oh, help…" She gave up and joined in the laughter. "Now what am I going to do?"

"What I've told you to do from the very start," Zach answered, a bit more serious but retaining the appealing twinkle in his eyes. "Take him home. Houdini's yours."

Chapter Eight

"Ah...*mio marito è pazzo!*" Mama shook her head. "My husband is crazy, like his daughter. We cannot take a dog. I have to care for you, Antonio, not pick up...up...oof! You know. Doggie mess is too much to worry about when you're sick still."

"But look at him," Papa argued, a broad smile on his lips. "He's happy, and I am, too. He comes home with us."

At Gabi's side, Zach snickered. "I told you so."

Swallow me, earth! "Oh, hush! We can't take Houdini home, and you know it. It doesn't make any sense to saddle Mama with more to do."

He crossed his arms and leaned a fraction away from her, studying her intently. "I agree. And that's why they have a lovely, competent daughter staying with them. She can take care of Houdini's training for a while."

"But I'm at Tony's all day, and I'm going back to my job in—"

"Cleveland, I know." His jaw tightened as he fell silent again.

He didn't seem to have liked the reminder, but it had needed to be said. She was going back…eventually. She turned toward her parents, who'd built up quite the disagreement over the dog. Papa, who was well-known for digging in his heels, was determined to keep Houdini.

Mama, no slouch in the stubbornness department either, refused to bring the dog home. As the argument dragged on, Gabi grew anxious. Papa wasn't supposed to put himself under a lot of stress. From the red tinge on his cheeks, which weren't sunburned since he and Mama had stayed under the extended roof over the entrance of the shelter building the whole morning, he looked plenty stressed to her.

In the midst of it all, and in spite of the commotion, Houdini had fallen sleep. He now let out a gentle snore. Papa absently stroked the terrier, who then settled back down and slept in peace again, while the older Carlinis argued his fate over his unconcerned head.

That broke through Gabi's resistance. It looked to her as though Houdini had won in the end. He'd picked his family. "Hey!" she called out in surrender. "Tell you what. How about if we take him home on one condition."

"What?" Mama said.

"Condition?" Papa's eyebrows rose. "What condition?"

"Whatever you've come up with," Zach said in a calm, quiet voice, "I'll help, and see that things go well with your parents, even after you leave."

She nodded, still facing her parents. "We'll give this a try, so long as everyone understands that if Houdini's not housebroken and reasonably trained by the time I leave, we'll have to find him a new home. That's where you'll come in, Zach."

"Deal!" he exclaimed at her side. "It'll never happen. That dog's going *home* to your parents' house, and that's where he's going to stay. He's smart, really smart, and I know you're going to be a great trainer. You'll see I'm right on this, too."

She flashed him a skeptical look. "Glad you're that sure. Especially since it's not up to you to make sure he succeeds."

"I just promised to help, didn't I?" Then he waved toward Papa. "But, look. You can't deny that dog's good for your father. It wouldn't make sense to keep fighting the inevitable."

"Wish I felt as confident as you do." She faced her mother. "Can you agree with my plan, Mama?"

Her mother looked from Papa to Gabi to the dog, and then the most reluctant smile she'd ever seen bloomed across her still-smooth cheeks. "Too many of you to argue with me for the dog. Very well.

Houdini comes home with us. But, Gabriella, it's up to you—"

"Mama! I'm not six years old anymore. Of course I'll take care of him."

Zach stepped toward the table, grabbed an adoption application and returned, his mouth covered with the form but failing to hide his laughter. "I suspect you were one mighty handful when you were little."

"That's what I've been told."

"Haven't changed a bit, then, have you?" he asked, handing her a pen and the papers.

She chuckled. "The jury's still out on that one."

"Not from what I can see." And with that, he walked away. "Remember," he called out as he went into the building again. "I promised to help. I plan to keep that promise."

A shot of pleasure went through her at the thought of seeing him more often. Maybe this whole dog adoption thing would work out after all. Maybe by the time she left she would have found something to really object to about Zach Davenport.

But she wasn't going to hold her breath.

Five days later, Zach showed up at Gabi's house, about an hour after she'd left Tony's. He knew her hours because he'd called and asked when she'd finished at the restaurant. He didn't know whether to laugh at his schoolboy antics or kick himself for being a sap. But one thing was for sure—this woman had captured his attention. At the least convenient time, too.

Her mother gave him a hug as he walked inside the Carlini home. She called up the stairs, "Gabriella! That nice Zach from the place for dogs is here for you. Come down."

A couple of minutes later, Gabi walked downstairs, towel-drying her hair. "Oh, hi," she said, and gave him a weak smile. "Sorry, I'm nowhere near at my best. There's just something about the smell of tomatoes, garlic and basil when I'm no longer at the restaurant that makes me rush to the nearest shower."

"You look fine." She looked cute, but he doubted she'd appreciate that assessment. "And you look far better than that poor critter we bathed the night before the fair."

She blushed, and when he realized what he'd just alluded to, he grimaced, afraid she'd beat a hasty retreat again. Instead, she just shook her head and smiled. "I don't know what to say about a man who compares me with a stray dog, but I guess I have to consider the source. So, did you need something?"

He shrugged and followed her into a tastefully decorated living room. He looked around at the caramel-toned upholstered furniture, the soft green walls and the cheerful splashes of the same green, some yellow and blue in a handful of pillows scattered around. "Nice," he said. "And no, I didn't come to stick my foot in my mouth, but rather to keep my promise. How's Houdini settling in?"

He hoped she could appreciate his ability to laugh at himself. When she grinned and sat in a comfortable-looking armchair, he relaxed a bit.

She gestured him toward the sofa. "I'm happily surprised. He's turned out to be even smarter than I realized, and far more obedient than I would have imagined, as stubborn as he is."

"He figured out right away how good he has it now."

She folded the towel and set it down on the side table. "Thanks. I really like him, too. I did from that first day when he was all dirty and stinky."

"And your dad? How's he doing with Houdini?"

"He's loving every minute he can spend with that dog. But I'm sure you expected that, too. After all, you took Papa's side against me the other day."

"Not really. I knew Houdini belonged with you the first time I laid eyes on the two of you. Then, when he took to your father the same way…well, that sealed the deal for me. Houdini had found his forever home with your family."

They both fell silent, and he had to scramble mentally to find something to talk about. "Ah…I haven't seen you at the shelter these last couple of days. I hope you haven't changed your mind about volunteering."

"Not at all. I've just been that busy sourcing the decor for the remodel of Tony's—Antonio's. And I've interviewed a couple of applicants, but that hasn't gone as well. Don't know why it's so hard to hire someone with the right qualifications."

His curiosity grew. "You mean for the chef?"

"And the manager, too. I could get back to my job if I hired a good manager. But I need someone who has solid experience hiring and firing staff. I need someone I can trust to find the right executive chef."

"I see." But he really didn't. The more Gabi insisted on her proposed changes, the more certain Zach grew she was on the wrong path. But he didn't want to start another battle with her. Maybe a different subject would be better, since biting his tongue to keep his opinion to himself was getting old.

"About Houdini," he began, getting back to the original purpose for his visit. "I had an idea I wanted to run past you, but first I had to know how he was working out."

"You've got my attention. Now that you've seen how well things are going, tell me what you're up to."

"I'm not up to anything—yet. I'd like to see if you'd be interested in training Houdini as a therapy dog. The idea first came to my mind at the Adoption Fair when I saw how well he related to your dad."

"Oh, now that's interesting." She leaned forward and propped her elbows on her knees, her chin on her hands. "What would it take for him to become a therapy dog?"

He couldn't stop the appreciative smile. Her keen interest embodied her lively personality. No wonder she drew him like a salmon onto a fisherman's bait off the well-known pier in nearby Edmonds.

He couldn't afford to swallow the hook. Better to focus on the dog. "He needs to become a certified Canine Good Citizen, and then go through a couple of other types of training, but we can start on the CGC. I'm AKC-approved as a CGC evaluator, so we can start to work on it right away."

"What makes a dog a Canine Good Citizen?"

"Well, you can train any dog to become one, but I prefer to start with one who has a good temperament. I think we can all agree Houdini's been blessed with that." At her enthusiastic nod, he went on. "Then he has to be socialized really well. We'll have to take him all kinds of places and expose him to all kinds of people. That's really important."

"He's a ham. He should do well around people."

"Exactly. And now that you've discovered he's such a quick learner, as well as obedient, then we have the second part of the inherent qualities sewed up, too."

"I'm sure his charmer talents will help him worm his way into people's hearts!"

"That's a given. He's had that beat from the first dive into Tony's Dumpster, don't you think?"

"I don't know about the Dumpster, but when I opened the door to see what was doing the scratching, he stole my heart right away."

Zach had to clamp his lips tight to keep from saying, *Lucky dog!*

He pasted on a more appropriate smile and continued, irritated by his easy susceptibility. "Now, we have to focus on the socialization. It's one of the most important components of the training. We'll have to decide what kind of events we want to take him to and what type of situations will help him with his good responses. That's easy to do, and then we can also start obedience training right away."

"We?"

"I'd like your help, especially since he's young and will be your family's dog for many, many years. Small terriers, as a general rule, have a long life expectancy. You'll want to teach your parents everything you and Houdini learn."

A touch of alarm widened her eyes, and he could see her putting up the usual roadblocks—her life back in Cleveland and her impending return there. "Will you be the one who'll take him to…what? Hospitals?" she asked. "The assisted-living facility down on Seagull Drive?"

He ground his teeth in frustration. Just as he'd been certain the dog belonged with her, or at least her family, he felt in his heart that she belonged in Lyndon Point. But it would do no good to push that point, not when she remained so dead set against staying.

"Sure, I can take him. But more important, the reason we want him certified as a CGC and a service dog is so your father can keep him at his side at all times. Once we get his certifications, Houdini will have a little red vest that identifies him as your father's helper, and no one can deny him entrance wherever your dad goes."

"You mean we take Houdini to doctor, grocery, or church?" Mama asked as she walked in carrying a loaded tray. "A dog?"

Zach rose and helped her set the heavy silver piece down on the coffee table in front of the sofa. "Yes, but a dog that's been trained so he can go to all kinds of different places."

"My Antonio will love it!"

Zach grinned. "I knew he would. That's why I came to talk to Gabi about it. I'm glad you joined us when you did, Mrs. Carlini."

"I think it's a great idea," Gabi said, stepping to the table. "And it's a great idea that you brought out your lemon-drop cookies, Mama. But you should have called me. I could have brought the tray in for you. I'm sure it was heavy."

On his way back to his seat, his elbow brushed against Gabi's arm, and he caught the way her eyes widened at the contact. For a moment, she paused and stared at the spot where they'd grazed, seemingly flustered by the feather-light skin-to-skin stroke.

It pleased Zach to know he wasn't the only one affected by their nearness. Before he could stop it, a dangerous thought crossed his mind. He wondered what it would be like if their relationship grew to where those touches were the norm between them rather than a moment to remember.

"Bah!" Mrs. Carlini said, pulling him away from his wild imagination. "Six weeks ago or so, I carried heavy trays of pizza and salads and pasta plates to the tables at Tony's. Now, I just take his plate to Antonio three times a day. This tray? Bah! *Non é niente*—it's nothing."

Zach tried to hide his chuckle. This was where Gabi got her zesty personality. He liked the Carlinis. What was there not to like?

"So we're all agreed, then?" he asked, just to make sure. "Houdini's going into training."

The two women answered yes, and then they all dived into the cookies and rich, dark coffee Mrs. Carlini had brought.

A time or two, as they enjoyed their refreshments, he caught Gabi sneaking glances in his direction, just as he had done toward her. The realization touched a cold spot inside him, and it began to thaw.

The surge of adrenaline that struck him at the top of a slalom slope made its appearance at that most unusual moment. Oh, sure. Gabi posed a danger to his equilibrium, but one he wasn't ready to flee. Good thing he'd followed through on his urge to see her again.

After Mrs. Carlini hurried away to see to her husband, he and Gabi settled in to talk and play a lively game of Clue. Even when hours had gone by, he didn't want to leave. To Zach, it felt like the perfect end to an almost perfect day.

Perfect would have been a day spent with Gabi. The perfect end would have been if she'd said she'd decided to move back home permanently.

And the perfect fool would be him, for wanting both of those impossible things.

Sunday after church, Gabi hurried to Tony's to make sure things were ready for the last day of the weekend rush. This was when they made most of their profit, from Friday after school let out until closing on Sunday evening.

They had always opened for a late lunch at two, encouraging their patrons to attend church services, and ever since she'd come back to Lyndon Point, she'd made it a point to help her employees prep ingredients for the salads, the pizza toppings and their most popular Italian dishes. As she finished at the last station—the garlic bread stop—she licked a dab of Papa's signature blend of olive oil and butter from her index finger. All the bread needed now was a sprinkle of fresh Parmesan and a quick pop under the broiler.

The hours flew by as they filled order after order. Later, her phone rang. "Hey, birthday girl!" Allie cried. "What are you doing to celebrate?"

"Birthday girl?" Gabi asked. "Celebrate? What day is it?"

"It's June fifteenth, woman! Are you Pacific Northwesters so laid-back that you don't even use calendars out there?"

Gabi leaned over to glance out the kitchen door to the cash register and was surprised to notice on the calendar that her best friend was right. It was her birthday, and she'd completely missed it.

"Guess the laugh's on me." She gave a quick look around to check if anyone else could see how sheepish she felt. "And to answer your question, I'm serving supper at Tony's. That's how I'm celebrating my birthday—"

"Not anymore, you're not!" Dylan loped up to her and took the phone from her hand. "You're outta here, boss. Now!"

"Hey! Give me that phone back."

"Okay. Here you go." The teen's grin was infectious. "And Allie's in on this, too, so she's already hung up. Your chariot awaits outside the door."

"What are you talking about?" she asked, but let him lead her toward the front of the restaurant. As she walked through the dining room, the customers broke into an off-key rendition of "Happy Birthday."

"Thanks," she murmured when they finished singing and clapping.

"You must go and have fun now, Gabriella!" Mama said, stepping out from behind the checkout counter. "You come home, help us so much. I want you to take break. Happy birthday, *mia dolce figlia,* my sweet girl."

Gabi's eyes welled as her mother gave her a warm hug and untied the apron she'd put on when she'd walked in right after church. Mama donned the tomato-smeared garment and pushed her daughter toward the door. "Claudia's at our home with Houdini and Papa," she added. "I'm here, and it's your birthday now. You go!"

Gabi felt more than a little disoriented. There were surprise birthday parties, and then there was… this. "You've all gone nuts!"

As she stepped outside and the door closed behind her, she spotted Zach standing next to a silver SUV parked in front of Tony's, his grin as wide as Dylan's. "Happy birthday."

"You're in on it, too?"

He shrugged and held the vehicle's door open for her. "Birthdays are for celebrating. Come on, let's go eat. I wouldn't want our meal to be less than at its best."

"Meal, huh?" She slid into the car. "Lucky for you, I'm really hungry."

He hurried around to the driver's side, then sat behind the wheel. "You've spent all afternoon at a pizza place, and you're actually hungry? There's something wrong with this picture."

"There's only so much pizza one woman can eat."

He maneuvered the car smoothly through the town's light Sunday evening traffic and then headed toward the north side of Lyndon Point. All the while she couldn't help stealing glances at his handsome profile and noticing how good he looked in his faded jeans and navy blue polo shirt. As they continued toward their destination, the neighborhood streets soon gave way to a winding road overlooking a stretch of empty coastline. He pulled into the parking area for a public beach and stopped next to boulders stacked high, about thirty or forty feet from the water.

"This is where we're eating?" she asked, confused. "I thought we were having a meal, something that had an optimal time to serve."

He shot her that mischievous grin she liked so much, topped with that appealing twinkle in his eyes. "You were listening to me."

"Of course I was. I always listen when I'm being kidnapped." She wrinkled her nose and gave him a crooked smile. "Anyway, what are we eating?"

"You'll see soon enough."

She was about to push, but he hopped out of the car and went to the liftgate before she could get even one word out. From the back of the car, he withdrew a large picnic basket and what looked like a white tablecloth.

"Are you nuts?" she asked. "Who brings nice white linens to the beach?"

"I do." He carried his load to the opening between the boulders that led to the beach. "Your birthday dinner calls for a few nice details. I'm happy to oblige."

"So what are we eating?" she tried again, hoping to catch him off guard.

"Uh-uh-uh! You'll have to show a bit of patience."

Both laughed, and she gave up. She was enjoying herself and was secretly thrilled he'd gone to all the trouble of arranging this. Or helping her mother arrange it—whichever way it had gone. She loved the thought he'd put into pleasing her.

She perched on the nearest rock to watch him set up for their meal. The more he did, the more he impressed her.

Soft breezes off the Puget Sound lifted the stray strands that had escaped her slicked-back ponytail and, after a day of work, now curled on her forehead. Since she no longer was at Tony's, she slipped off the elastic she used to hold her thick hair out of her way while she worked and ran her fingers through it. The release felt wonderful, and for the first time in a long time, she began to relax.

As she raked the mass back out of her face, she noticed how low the sun had dropped on the horizon. It was much later than she'd thought. Since she wasn't wearing a watch, and she didn't feel like going to get her smartphone from the car to check the time, she decided to let the day measure the hours for her.

"This was a good idea," she called out to Zach.

He grinned back. "I know. And it was all mine."

"But I gather my mother helped."

"Sure. I needed help getting it all set up."

No surprise there. After all, Zach was handsome, charming, gainfully employed and—most important in her mother's eyes—a happy resident of Lyndon Point. Mama had muttered something about babies the day of the Adoption Fair. And she never failed to mention all the various cousins who were loving life with their kids.

The back-and-forth rush of the waves on the gritty, water-ground rock that made up the beach's rough sand began to lull her into a state close to bliss. If she separated her hometown from her bad memories, there was a lot to like about it.

There were those relatives who'd insisted she become a nurse, a physical therapist or a doctor, of course. Others had pushed for academia, suggesting archeology, ornithology or even herpetology. Never mind how much she hated dirt, sand and even the idea of ancient bones, how birds of all kinds creeped her out and her profound hatred of snakes. Worst of all were the ones who'd insisted the best thing for her to do was to find herself a good Lyndon Point boy, settle down with him and get busy adding to their vastly spreading family.

Few of them listened long enough to hear what mattered most to her, and while Mama and Papa understood her interest in pursuing her education, they never failed to remind her of the University of Washington, which was located in their proverbial backyard, nearby Seattle.

The pressure to become what they wanted, rather than the woman God had created her to be, grew to suffocate her. The memories of the discussions— according to them, battles according to her—still made her antsy. Her love for her relatives made it difficult to think of Lyndon Point and her family as two separate entities.

In her mind, they were too intricately connected, too tightly entwined for her to set apart. Too bad she couldn't do that kind of separating. And her independence had come at the cost of a lot of effort. She couldn't forget that, even if Lyndon Point's picturesque beauty could make forgetting an easy thing.

"All set!" Zach called. "Come join me."

Gabi opened her eyes again and picked her way over the boulders down to the waterfront, where he'd set a beautiful scene. "Oh, my! Plates, serving dishes, that sparkling white tablecloth. You thought of everything."

"I aim to please, ma'am, if I can use an ancient cliché. You really do like it? And nobody let you in on the plan?"

"Are you kidding me? I had no idea. If I'd known you'd planned something as beautiful as this for me, I wouldn't have been wrapped in a tomato-splattered apron, and with garlic-daubed fingers to boot, when you got there."

He sat on one corner of the white tablecloth and held out a hand. "I'll take the fun of your surprise and count my blessings there, even when they come Italian-scented."

She swatted at his comment but did take his hand. She sat at his side to admire his handiwork. He'd set the tablecloth with a pair of silver-edged white plates that looked elegant and expensive. In the center of each, he'd placed a fan-folded napkin, and at each side he'd arranged the proper silverware—each piece gleaming in the persimmon light of dusk. A pair of large water goblets brimming with amber-toned iced tea sat precariously in front of each place setting.

She leaned forward right away. "Oh, hey! We'd better pick these up before the breeze knocks them over. It's pretty warm still, and we don't want to go thirsty."

He glanced at the horizon. "Sun's almost all the way down, so it won't be as hot for too much longer. But how about if you hold mine, too? I have to get one more detail I almost forgot."

She grabbed the two goblets, and watched him rummage in the large basket. To her amazement, he brought out a small glass hurricane lamp with a marble bottom and a chunky, pristine-white candle. "Wow! I wasn't kidding when I said you'd thought of everything."

He flashed her that terrific smile of his but didn't say anything as he used a long-handled gas lighter. "There. At least it won't be pitch-dark while we eat."

"I didn't realize how late it was. I thought it was only around five when you got to Tony's."

"Think again." He gestured toward the stunning sunset. "It was closer to seven. We're lucky we're in mid-June and the sun doesn't completely set until quite late."

"So what did you bring to fill my growling belly?"

"First we're having caramelized pecan, pear and arugula salad with raspberry balsamic vinaigrette."

He'd gone all-out. "That sounds delicious. I'm ready."

Zach withdrew a small insulated container from the picnic box and, with silver salad tongs, served them each a lovely mound of fresh greens, golden-browned pears and toasted pecans from individual sections. He then drizzled the dressing over it all.

"Let's pray," he murmured, holding out his hand.

She smiled, nodded and placed her fingers in his. As he enfolded them in his strong clasp, a sense of peace filled her. She let all her other thoughts vanish with the dropping sun. What a lovely way to celebrate her birthday.

"Heavenly Father," Zach said, "bless the food You've given us, and bless this evening we're about to share. Father, bring Gabi joy in this next year of her life, bless her with all the riches of Your glory. In Your precious Son's name, I pray…"

"Amen," she breathed. He echoed her, and then she immediately forked up a mouthful of the glistening greens. "Yum…"

"Do you like it?"

"Love it!" She jabbed the fork over her shoulder. "A few minutes ago while I was sitting on the rock, I thought the salty breezes and the sound of the waves made the evening feel something akin to bliss, but compared to this, it doesn't even come close."

"Great! Enjoy."

They ate, discussing a number of light subjects, from the new exhibit at the Lyndon Point Historical Society to Houdini's latest antics while training for his Canine Good Citizen. When they'd finished their salads, he brought out a two-person crockery-type heated carrier and served them rosy-toned slabs of rosemary-sprigged roast leg of lamb and tender multicolored new potatoes. Next to all that bounty, he piled grilled zucchini, red and yellow peppers and sliced Portobello mushrooms, then sprinkled the vegetables with creamy feta cheese.

"What a feast! I feel as though I'm at a five-star restaurant in downtown Seattle," she said after she'd tasted the melt-in-your-mouth lamb. "Am I dreaming?"

"Nope. You're just celebrating your birthday out in God's nicest dining room."

In spite of herself and the measure of greater wisdom she knew she had, she could feel herself falling deeper for his irresistible appeal. At the rate she was going, heartbreak wasn't going to be the inevitable end to all this. Obliteration of her heart was where she was headed.

What a way to go. Maybe...

But no. She'd always believed God's best for her was in Ohio, not in Lyndon Point. It was time to enjoy what she should and forget the riskier maybes.

By the time she thought she couldn't eat another morsel, Zach surprised her with the most spectacular part of the meal. "Since a regular birthday cake wouldn't travel too well," he said, "we have my favorite dessert—a Dobos torte."

She winked. "That sounds *très, très* fancy."

He shrugged as he set before her a clear plastic container with a many-layered pastry inside. A pair of dessert plates followed. "It's originally Hungarian, but it's become international by now. I think you're going to love it."

Moments later, after she'd had her first bite, she smiled in delight. "Looks like I have a brand-new favorite dessert. What's in it?"

"It's made of layers of sponge cake, layers of chocolate buttercream and topped with very thin slices of caramel."

After she swallowed again, she pointed at him with her fork. "I told you you're a foodie. I was right."

"I love to eat, so why bother eating something that's not exceptional?"

"Makes perfect sense to me." She took another bite and, as she savored this one more slowly, an idea began to take form. "This is exactly what I'm looking for, you know, but in a distinctly Italian vein. I would appreciate the name of the restaurant where you bought this. I need to hire this chef away from wherever he's working. Please tell me where this wonderful meal came from."

To her complete shock, Zach dropped his fork onto his plate, the loud clatter suggesting a possibly broken piece of the expensive china.

Uh-oh. What had she done wrong? Was it something she'd said?

Chapter Nine

This was exactly what he'd feared when he'd thought up the unconventional birthday celebration. He'd known he would run the chance of exposing his background by cooking for her, but he'd wanted to do something special for her, something no one else could do.

And yet, he'd also known he couldn't tell her how personal a gift the meal was. However, he'd never expected her to take this route. He'd never thought she'd want to hire the unknown chef.

"Uh, it's getting late," he murmured, unable to meet her gaze. "Besides, I think you're barking up the wrong tree with that gourmet restaurant idea of yours. Think of the yawning gap you'll leave in the town once you take away the local pizza hangout."

She clenched her jaw, then shook her head "Not really. No one's taking Birdie's Nest away from the town, so they'll still have a hangout. The Nest offers a great menu, and no one *needs* pizza to hang out. I have to think of my family's well-being first."

Gabi seemed determined to remain willfully blind. Still, he had to try to make her see reason. "So you've said from the start, but I don't think you've considered what this would mean to local families. They need a choice, and even though the diner is fine for the adult crowd, and maybe even the older teens, I don't see as many little kids there as I do at Tony's. Your parents have worked hard to create a welcoming, homey atmosphere, and pizza is a natural draw for kids. That means families, and families mean steady business."

"I'm sorry, Zach." She stood. "I think it's best for us to agree to disagree on this. But I am tired now." She shook off the gritty beach sand from her flip-flops and slipped them back on. "I do thank you for the loveliest birthday celebration ever, and I would appreciate the name of the chef or, at the very least, where you bought the food."

He shook out the tablecloth, folded it and picked up the repacked basket. Walking back to the car, he pretended not to have heard her repeated request. Why had he ever thought he could get away with this? It had never occurred to him that she might ask who'd made the food—but it should have. He'd been too busy thinking of her in personal terms rather than as the driven career woman she was.

He should have left that kind of infatuated thinking behind ages ago. But there was just something about Gabi Carlini that sent common sense flying right out of his head. Now the memory she'd have of her birthday was of an argument instead of a romantic time.

No wonder he was still single.

They returned to town in silence. He pulled up in front of her home, then dashed around the car to let her out. They walked to the house without speaking a word, and he again felt like a gawky junior high boy.

"Thanks," she said in a voice so soft he had to strain to catch her words. "It really was wonderful. No one's ever done something so sweet and thoughtful for me."

"Really?" He leaned a hip against the wrought-iron banister on the broad front stoop. "Do you only hang out with men who are idiots?"

She turned toward him and arched a delicate eyebrow.

He bit down on his tongue, wishing he were more polished and suave. "As you can tell, I'm a man who chews shoe leather on a regular basis." He shook his head at his own awkwardness. "I'm just surprised that having someone do something nice like this would strike you as so unusually special."

"I haven't dated much over the years." She stuck her hand in her pocket, and as she drew out the key, it caught the scant light and sparkled, much like the sparkle he'd come to expect from her. The sparkle that was now missing from her expression.

He called himself more kinds of fool and was about to change the subject, but she beat him to the draw, continuing the touchy conversation.

"I was always the bookworm kind," she said. "Worse yet, I was the girl who did better at math and science than the guys did. After college, I've done nothing but work like crazy, and that seems to be the kiss of death when it comes to men. Having little time to worry about a social life makes it easier not to feel crummy about it."

"It's not the kiss of death in my book. I like a smart woman. Especially one that's as beautiful as she is smart. Like you."

Her eyes opened wide, and in the golden glow of the single light hanging from the front-stoop overhang, he saw her cheeks turn pink. He'd noticed before how easily she blushed, and he liked that in her. It showed she wasn't nearly as tough as she tried to portray herself.

She blinked up at him a couple of times, and he was glad he wasn't the only one who felt ill at ease at a private moment like this. It gave him hope where he shouldn't have any hope at all. But, still, it did.

She rubbed her palms against her denim shorts, dropped the key, then hurried to pick it up before he did. "I—I don't know what to say."

He smiled and placed his hands on her shoulders,

making her look at him again. "You don't have to say a word."

Even though he knew he would regret it, probably sooner rather than later, he leaned down and placed a tender kiss on her lips. Under his touch, he felt her gentle tremor.

The light caress moved him as much as it did her. Everything in him wanted to hold her to him, to kiss her again and again, to whisper sweet things that would help her see how appealing she was, but he called on every ounce of his self-discipline and simply ran a finger down her soft cheek.

He wanted to stay close to her, just like that, and bare his soul to her, but he couldn't. Sensing it would be better to keep things light, he stepped away with another gentle touch to her cheek. "Thanks for coming with me. I'd love to do something like this again sometime."

He turned and started back down the front walk toward his car, then paused. With a glance over his shoulder, he saw her lift her hand to her mouth, softly rub where his lips had touched hers, and smile.

In spite of her smile, she looked stunned, but in a good way. He couldn't smother his own responding grin. "Good night, Gabi."

By the time he drove away, he realized he'd begun to whistle a sappy old show tune. Oh, yeah. He did have it bad. And it was only getting worse.

He wondered what Gabi thought about him now.

* * *

The days after her birthday flew by in a hectic whirl. And her emotions spun in an equally dizzy blur after Zach's good-night kiss. Wow! Who would have thought such a brief moment of contact could pack such a powerful punch?

On Wednesday, the church's youth group descended on Tony's as they usually did after they'd been dismissed. As always, pitchers of soda and pepperoni pizzas zipped from behind the counter and onto the tables with stunning speed. By the time the kids' curfew rolled around, Gabi was sick of tomatoes and oregano, and exhausted, too.

She started to clean up and was about to throw out the last six slices that remained in the kitchen when she heard the beep of the electronic motion sensor on the front door. Male voices rumbled, and then she heard Dylan come back her way.

"Hey, boss. Are you up to making another pizza or do we have enough to feed a hungry guy?"

Without looking up, she sprinkled scouring powder on baked-hard sauce in the corner of the lasagna pan she'd just dunked in the steel sink. "Who's out there?"

"Zach just got here. Says he never had a chance to pick anything up at the Nest, and they're closed by now. Can we take care of him?"

At the mention of his name, Gabi dropped the pan with a clatter, rinsed her hands and dried off on a clean towel. "Of course. Why don't you go on home. I—I can take care of his order. Um…you've been here since early today, and I can find someone to help me close up."

How could the man make her so flustered? Just by walking into the restaurant like dozens of people did every day?

Dylan didn't immediately leave. "Are you sure?" he asked.

When she nodded, he shrugged. "If you say so. And thanks. See you in the morning."

She placed the pizza slices in the oven to run them through only long enough to warm them and crisp the crusts again. "Oh, and on your way out, have Sarah take Zach's drink order."

"Will do. See you tomorrow."

Gabi hurried to the cooler for the makings of a salad, the new one she hoped would soon turn into the signature starter for the new Antonio's. As soon as she opened the veggie crispers, though, she groaned. A ton of the fresh greens were still there, just as had been the case the past two days. Maybe she'd have to adjust her order downward. Again.

She plated up a vibrant mix of field greens, cucumber slices, yellow heirloom tomatoes, radish slivers and a small cluster of dried cherries. On her way out, she snagged a condiment carrier with bottles of olive oil and balsamic vinegar. As she walked toward Zach, she lectured herself on how to approach him without making a fool of herself. It didn't help much, since when she reached his side, she felt as flustered—oh, yes—as a smitten schoolgirl. "Hi."

He met her gaze when she placed his food before him. "I didn't expect to see you here this late."

She looked away, the memory of the kiss vivid as ever. "It was my turn on our new schedule rotation."

He drizzled vinegar and oil on his salad, and then, when he took a bite, his expression changed. "Oh. I hadn't paid any attention to what you'd given me. I'm surprised. I thought you always served chopped romaine. What's with the mixed field greens?"

"I figured we'd better start upscaling the menu so that when the changeover happens our customers will be somewhat prepared."

He gave her a sideways look, and she felt the worst urge to squirm, but she squashed it.

"How's that going?"

"I was afraid you'd ask."

His eyebrow arched. "That good?"

She couldn't evade the question again. "We have a bit of waste in the trash bins."

"A bit?" He shook his head. "These greens are a lot more fragile than good old romaine. There's a reason it's a staple in so many restaurants."

She shrugged. To her relief, the timer she'd set in the kitchen went off. "I'll be right back with your pizza."

She almost groaned at herself as she hurried back. *Cowardice, thy name is Gabriella*. Since she couldn't very well hide out in the kitchen, she brought Zach's steaming food right out. As she approached the table again, she noticed Sarah still hanging around behind the counter, her gaze firmly fixed on the wall clock.

"Go ahead," she told the girl. "I'll close up. Zach's the only one here, and I can finish what cleanup is left."

She locked up behind the teen, and, since there was no polite way to avoid it, she went and sat across from Zach.

"Okay if I join you?" she asked, even though she would much rather have scrubbed out gross trash cans than face the possibility of rehashing their differences or revisiting that powerful kiss.

"I'd be pretty disappointed if you didn't." He munched away, washed the bite down with soda and then looked back up at her. "So…tell me. How are the customers responding to the change in salads?"

And stubbornness, thy name is Zach. "Not as well as I would have hoped. At least, not yet. I think they need more time. Plus a good chef who would make up a tastier dressing than just balsamic and oil."

"Have you had any complaints? Salads returned to the kitchen?"

She grimaced. "One complaint about the 'pasture

on the plate,' and two untouched salads returned and refunded."

"What's this going to do to your profits?"

"That's my greatest fear. You know the new greens and the fancier vegetables are pricier than plain stuff, so I'm going to see a difference pretty quickly here if I have to refund a whole lot more."

"I'm sorry."

"What about?" She took in a long, slow breath and braced herself for whatever he might say.

"I did try to warn you. Delicate greens are more appropriate for Seattle or trendier towns like Edmonds. Lyndon Point is more family-oriented. Sturdy and cheaper romaine and beefsteak tomatoes mean a better margin for you."

With a blunt fingernail, she drew a circle on a paper napkin she'd grabbed to have something to keep her hands busy. "But I can't charge as much for romaine as I can for arugula and radicchio. I need the higher profit margin of the upgraded greens to increase that tiny margin as much as possible."

Zach shook his head. "You'll lose that much more when you throw out the more expensive ingredients the customers don't like."

Gabi remained determined to stand for what she believed was best for her family. "People will love them the more they eat them."

"It's not working, and it's not going to. You need to see that before you make a mistake you can't fix."

She huffed out a frustrated breath. "So, tell me. Who made you such an expert?"

He reared back in the booth, and a pained expression etched twin lines between his brows. "Personal experience."

"Personal?"

"Firsthand personal. The been-there, done-that kind of experience."

She felt like Alice on her way down the rabbit hole. "What do you mean you have *personal experience?* What kind of expertise can a shelter guy have with salad greens, profit margins and family pizzerias?"

"I have plenty of experience with all of the above—take your pick." He pushed away his by-now cold pizza and stared at his hands.

"Go for it," she challenged. "Tell me all about it."

In a monotone voice, he spoke about years spent in the food industry, a number of prestigious culinary schools attended and then more dues paid climbing the ladder until he reached the peak of his field and opened up his own multi-star-reviewed gourmet restaurant.

Never in a million years would she have imagined it, although she should have suspected something after her birthday picnic. Still, he could have blown her away by waving a feather in her face.

But then, his story took a turn for the worse. In a voice rough with pain, he told her how a load of produce from his regular organic supplier had come tainted with salmonella.

Oh, no! The moment he uttered the word, she wanted to stop him, to cover his hands with hers, to keep him from going over the inevitable end to his story. But he seemed so far away from her that she doubted he'd even hear her or feel her touch. She had to let him go on, no matter how much her heart responded to his misery, how much she wished she could spare him renewed pain.

As he described the vicious attacks of the media, tears stung the back of her eyelids. Her heart ached for Zach, and she realized she'd reached a new level of involvement. She'd come to care too much for him, but it was nothing she could change now.

He was a good man to whom a terrible thing had happened, one who still bore the scars. That deep need to comfort him magnified inside her. However, she knew that the best thing she could do for him was to listen to his pain-filled words.

He rapped his knuckles against the red laminate-topped table. "When I saw the listing for the position at the shelter," he said as he summed up his heartbreak at the accusations, the health inspections, the flight of patrons and the eventual death of his dream, "I knew it was an answer to prayer. It was as far from a kitchen as I could get, and I like it that way. I could never again risk sending another person to a hospital because of something I served them to eat. Never."

Gabi finally followed her instincts and covered his hands with hers. "I'm so sorry, Zach. I can't say I know just what you feel, but I can see how deeply it affects you, how much pain it brought you."

He met her gaze. "I've never felt so alone in my life. I lost even those I thought were my friends. From the way they reacted, you would have thought I'd pulled an Arsenic and Old Lace stunt."

She huffed. "Those weren't friends, then. You've told me what happened. You've told me people got very, very ill, and I'm not going anywhere. I'm not afraid of you, and anytime you want to feed me again, I'm in. You just needed better friends."

Although his grin was weak, it was a grin, and Gabi was glad to count it as a small victory.

"Thanks." He turned his hands over and laced his fingers through hers. "It's taken some time to get my feet back under me, but Lyndon Point's the best thing that's happened to me in a very long time."

The contrast between her experiences in her hometown—the smothering closeness of her enormous family, their determined nosiness, their relentless and unrequested advice, all of which had added to the ridicule of her peers—and his was stark and pointed. Lucky for him, and not so much for her.

She chose to focus on him. "I'm glad things are

better now. You've been given something not a lot of people get—a second chance."

"The shelter is a great fit for me. I've always loved animals, and I'm glad I can make a difference. Like tonight."

"Tonight?"

"That's why I'm eating so late." He shook his head, lips tight with disgust. "I got a call from Animal Control at around five. They'd had a report of an animal hoarder fifteen miles away. Wanted to know if we had room for a bunch of rescues." He exhaled wearily. "Thank goodness we had so many adoptions at the fair, and the shelter could accommodate them. Claudia and I drove out to give them a hand gathering all those poor cats—sixty-five of them. Some were feral, and all were in need of medical attention of one kind or another."

"How awful. I've heard about that kind of situation. Was it as bad as they show on TV?"

"I think it was worse. These were cats I could actually touch."

Gabi shuddered at the thought of the needy animals. "I get it. There's a degree of separation when you see it on a screen."

Zach let out a humorless chuckle. "You should have seen Claudia. She was steaming mad. If the man hadn't already been charged with animal cruelty and sent off with the cops, I think she would have taken him apart with her bare hands."

She grinned. "I can imagine. She's fierce."

"I'm blessed I can do something about that kind of cruelty, even if it's only on a local scale."

"You're blessed with an abundance of talents," she said, correcting him. Then, with a breath for courage, she decided to speak her heart. "Look at yourself. Not many people can shine in as many ways as you do. I don't think you should shut the door on your culinary gifts, no matter how good you are at the shelter and how much you love animals. Now that some time has passed since the trauma you suffered, maybe you can start to think about resuming your career."

He shook his head, his mouth set in a grim line. "I'm done with all that. These days, I stick to cooking for myself when I have the time—" he looked directly at her "—or making special birthday feasts for a special lady."

A warm, happy sensation filled her. "Thanks, but I don't think just because something horrible happened to you once, something over which you had no control, you need to turn your back on a career you loved."

He frowned. "Weren't you listening to me? People wound up in the hospital," he said, jabbing his index finger against the hard table, "some in critical condition, even—two senior citizens—because of me. I'm not doing that again. Not ever."

She couldn't let him continue to deny a gift like

his. She tried again. "I understand what you're saying, and I know firsthand how good you are at what you do at the shelter, but a talent like yours in the kitchen is not something to deny. God didn't bless you with it just so you could turn your back on it."

"I didn't just turn my back on it. I thought it through long and hard. I'm not going back there."

"Okay. I can understand your reluctance to going back to Sacramento. Especially since you like Lyndon Point so much. You can start over right here in town."

He flexed his jaw. "I just told you. I've started over. At the shelter."

"No…" She drew out the word, her mind barreling in all directions at warp speed. The thoughts came at her in vivid colors, bringing her ideas, possibilities, answers to her most fervent prayers. "That's not what I meant. You can start over here… as a chef. I believe things do happen for a reason, and that's why I think this is all so right."

He looked confused. "What are you talking about?"

"Well, you've begun to heal, haven't you?"

His shrug looked less than even halfhearted. "I suppose."

"And I can vouch for your culinary gifts. My birthday dinner was the best meal I've ever had—sorry, Mama."

Zach answered her compliment with another of those weak grins.

"Well, Chef Zach, I have the answer." She swept her arm through the air, indicating the dining room. "I need you here. I need the best chef in the world, and he's sitting across from me. You're hired."

As though she'd dumped a bucket of ice-filled water down his back, he reared up and out of the booth. Fury twisted his features, and anger blazed from his eyes.

"You didn't listen to a word I said, did you? Not one single thing. No, Gabi. I will not take your job. I will not go back to cooking for a living. I will never be a chef again, and you never should have thought I would. Not even for the briefest of moments."

She rose as well. "But it makes perfect sense! Listen to me. You know all about running a restaurant—you said you had great success until someone sold you infected lettuce. What are the odds you'll wind up with infected lettuce ever again? Besides, I need your help."

He crossed to the exit. "Please unlock this door for me. I'm done."

"Come on, Zach. I need—"

"How about you think about what someone else needs for a change? Your parents need you here, and I need peace of mind. You're not the only one who needs something." He glared at her. "Let me out of here, now."

From the set of his shoulders and the jutted angle of his jaw, Gabi saw he meant it. She'd never imagined he could get so mad. Certainly not by her offering him a job. And to insinuate she was unconcerned about her parents' needs? She was here, wasn't she?

"Fine," she groused. "Go. But I know you'll think about it. You won't be able to forget my offer just like that. It's a good one, and it makes more sense than anything else you've said."

Another of those heated glares came her way. "I hope you don't forget what *I* said, either. So many people in this town care about you. Not to mention that you have this great big loving family that keeps coming out of every corner, and they all want nothing more than to have you around." He shook his head in bewilderment. "I don't get you. Even after the health scare your father suffered, all you can think about is yourself, and your need for...for what? What are you still trying to prove, Gabi?"

She gasped. "How dare you?"

"I dare because I care, especially about your mom and dad. Their hearts will be broken when you take off again, just like mine was broken when my dream died. I know what it means to hurt. Don't hurt them. Think about them. And think about what you've just asked me to do."

He was right about one thing—the conversation was over. She unlocked the door and watched him stomp out. He left without saying another word.

Still, she doubted she'd be able to do anything but think for hours to come. And she had to wonder if she had anyone to blame but herself.

Could he be right…about *everything*?

Chapter Ten

"Hey, Zach," Claudia said in an uncharacteristically subdued voice as she walked into the tiny, cramped room they called his office. "The mayor's here, and he wants to see you. He has a big, fat folder under his arm, and looks pretty serious."

Although Zach wasn't someone who grew alarmed at the slightest thing, the unexpected nature of the visit—not to mention, the visitor himself—plus the expression on Claudia's face added up to an uneasy knot in his stomach. "Send him on back."

He always tried to keep his desk as clear as possible, but the maze of organizational baskets, shelves and trays—all full—made the top look like a mad scientist's rat-testing labyrinth. He hurried to gather up the papers he'd spread over the small patch of open space he kept at the front, snagged the stack of printouts he'd piled on the extra chair and stashed it all on top of his already crowded file cabinet.

In a perfect world, the shelter would be big enough to include an examination room for when the vet came to volunteer his services, and have a much larger kennel, a more spacious visitation play room and a more expansive storage area. But it wasn't a perfect world, and he'd become pretty good at making do.

"Hi, Zach," Ryder Lyndon said a few minutes later. "I see you have a full house again."

Zach briefly explained about getting a call regarding a hoarder in the area, helping Animal Control gather up dozens and dozens of cats, and bringing a number of them here. "All the other shelter facilities in the area are participating in the rescue as best they can," he said at the tail end of his account.

"You're doing great work."

Something about the grim way the mayor said those words sent dread straight to Zach's gut. That wasn't the expression one wore when complimenting someone on their success.

"How about if we cut through the chitchat," he said, unwilling to prolong the strained exchange. "If you'd like some coffee, Claudia makes a mean pot, and it's always fresh. Otherwise, let's get to the reason for your visit. I'm sure you have one."

Ryder gave a sharp nod, then opened the folder he'd carried. "You know the budget committee met last night, don't you?"

"I heard something about it, and I meant to attend

the general part of the town council's meeting, as I usually do, but after the influx of animals from the hoarder situation, we've had to play catch-up ever since."

"That's understandable." Ryder pulled out a sheet of paper and held it out to Zach. "This is the town's projected budget for the next fiscal year, which, as you know, starts August first. Take a look at the bottom line, especially in comparison with last year's, which we matched up item by item right next to it."

The picture presented by the figures was a grim one but not really surprising. "It looks like the economy is taking a bite out of the town's finances, just like it has with the rest of the country."

While Zach wasn't surprised, a disastrous possibility was starting to take root at the back of his mind. He refused to let it and waited for the mayor to go on.

Ryder did. "With so many residents struggling— mortgage issues, budget cuts with employers, layoffs and lackluster investment income—our tax revenues are way down. We have to pull in our belts just like everyone else, and there are a number of programs we're being forced to trim."

The possibility became a reality, but Zach still hoped against hope. "We can tighten our budget to match the rest of the town's cuts."

Ryder gave a tense shake of his head. "That's what I fought for last night, and it got nasty toward the end, everyone else fighting against me. I got the bad end of that one, since I argued with my heart instead of my calculator, as they all did." Looking like he'd been through the wringer, he scrubbed a hand across his face. "The reality is this—we're going to have to eliminate the funding for a number of good programs, and the shelter is one of them. The Historical Society is, too, and you know how that one went over with my wife."

Zach knew that Lucie, Ryder's wife, had bought the Victorian mansion at the corner of Sea Breeze Way and Main Street because of her love of history and her interest in preserving old architecture. "I can imagine."

"Yeah, well, the chill is in the air at home, and since we're beginning to hit the midsummer highs on the thermometer, you can figure out where I'm standing. I have a lot of charming to do, which will be fun, but not the issue here."

"No, the shelter is."

"Exactly." Ryder closed the folder with a slap that spoke of finality. "Unless you're able to raise the money to run the place on your own, and can continue to pay a reasonable rent to the town, then it's going to have to close. Lyndon Point just can't afford what it's costing us to fund it."

And Zach had just taken in a kennelful of new rescues who had nowhere else to go in the immediate future. The knot in his gut now felt more like a raging fire. How could this be happening to him?

"I'll put my head together with Claudia," he muttered, "and see what we can come up with."

In spite of his imminent panic, ideas rushed into his head. "We can contact a number of professional fundraising firms, and while we can't afford to hire them outright, maybe they can refer us to government programs that might help. We'll also contact the state, but I know what that budget shortfall looks like, so I doubt we'll find help there."

Ryder gave him an encouraging smile. "Glad to see you're not ready to give up."

Zach shrugged. "You saw the cages. What am I supposed to do? Let them all loose to run wild again?" He shook his head. "Can't do it. It wouldn't be right."

"I wish there was more I could do besides write you the biggest personal check Lucie and I can come up with. But the town council tied my hands."

"I appreciate you telling me that, and I understand your limitation. But I will take that check anytime you want to bring it down here."

The men shook hands, and Ryder crossed to the door, his steps as heavy as Zach's heart now felt. Panic threatened again, but he couldn't let it override his common sense. He turned to the Lord in a quick prayer for guidance and strength. Numerous responsibilities rested on his shoulders, and he had to keep his head straight to figure out what to do. He needed godly wisdom, maybe more than he ever had before.

As Ryder closed the office door, Zach's thoughts flew to the animals and his employees. The first thing to do was to meet with Claudia and Oscar. The second thing would be to log in time on the internet, scoping out government programs and non-profit foundations that might offer him hope for the animals' future. He wasn't about to give up without giving it everything he had.

A half hour later, after he'd broken the news to his staff, satisfaction and pride filled him. While new dollars to keep the Lyndon Point Animal Shelter going might never materialize, he now knew he'd built something special in the short time he'd been in town.

"You need to give me more credit," Claudia said, as she stepped away from the quick hug she gave him. "I'm in on this ride with you, no matter where it goes. We've worked too hard to quit at the first serious hurdle we face."

Oscar grinned, too. "I've never backed away from a challenge, and I get along with my pension and social security check just fine. Call my next paycheck a donation."

Zach thanked the older man, stunned by the generosity.

"Nah," Oscar said. "I'm not being all that generous. What would I do with myself if this place closed down? I'm not about to move into the fancy-pants assisted-living center down the road. I'm not ready to spend my days playing dominoes with a bunch of geezers—" he winked "—who are way too old for me."

Claudia went on to spill news of her own. "Timing's everything, isn't it?" she said. "Rick had a chance to apply for a pilot position with that small regional airline that runs flights to out-of-the-way locations in Alaska, and they called to offer it to him late last night. He's excited about the job and that he can spend more time at home with the kids."

"What will that mean for your family finances?" Zach asked.

"Not much, other than that he's retiring from the navy—he's put in twenty-four years—and he's starting something new. He'll be flying for a private company instead of for the navy. I can tighten up the belt, and you can keep my salary for the shelter." She gave him an exaggerated frown. "Until we get this joint back on its feet, you understand."

"Trust me. I want to pay you what you're both really worth. And I will, as soon as possible."

"We shouldn't take much of a hit," Claudia added. "I can cut a few luxuries like the designer coffee drinks and any extra vacation trips this year. I'm not about to run out on you, Zach. Not on you, not on the animals and not on Lyndon Point. The town needs the animal shelter."

He looked down the kennel aisle and nodded. "Then, team, let's roll up our sleeves and see what we can do."

As he turned toward his desk again, he began to pray. Nothing much would happen until he'd spent some serious time with God. Rough as his previous mess had been, he'd never felt abandoned by the Heavenly Father, even when he hadn't been able to see Him at work in his situation. He recognized that whatever happened in the future would only be easier to survive if he stayed close to God.

"Anything yet?" Claudia asked the next Monday morning.

Zach had spent the weekend glued to his laptop, researching foundations and philanthropies, as well as any and all possible government agencies and any applicable nongovernmental ones, too.

"I've sent out a couple of feelers, but our timing isn't as good as yours and Rick's. Most of these organizations make the decisions to allocate their funds the previous year. The ones I've spoken to would like to help, but they're flat out of cash."

Claudia grimaced. "I did write a good letter for our fund-raising appeal. Hopefully, the response will swamp us."

"Don't hold your breath."

"I never do. I prefer to keep swimming toward the shore."

"I'll be right there with you."

Oscar came into the room, his face in its usual calm lines. "I had an idea, Zach. I've heard many of the smaller, independent pet food manufacturers sometimes donate their product to operations like ours in exchange for publicity. Have you thought of contacting any of them? That would help with our overall costs."

"Do you mean something along the lines of sponsorships? And they'd be willing to cover the food bill in exchange for promotion?"

"That's what I mean."

"Hadn't thought of it, but I'll look into it. With as many pet food recalls as there have been in the past few years, more and more of those small food producers are popping up. I'd like to help them, especially if doing so will also help us."

"Let me know what happens." Oscar headed back to the kennels that needed to be hosed down before the shelter opened for business. That left Zach and Claudia in the office, both staring at the stack of bills on the desk. On top lay the one for the rent.

"What's going on with that?" she asked.

"Don't ask. It's not good. But I haven't given up."

She gave him another of her skeptical looks but didn't push it any further. She followed Oscar, since she had plenty to do before she unlocked the door for the day.

Now Zach was alone in the office with the bills, the rotten situation and his thoughts. Where did he go from here? He'd barely started to breathe again after his disaster in Sacramento, and now this. He'd prayed and prayed all weekend long, but God hadn't seen fit to bless him with any sudden flashes of wisdom.

"Hey," Gabi said from the door. "Am I interrupting?"

"Only my lousy thoughts." He paused, the memory of their last encounter too fresh in his mind. And, from the way she twisted her fingers and gnawed on her bottom lip, he didn't doubt it was in hers, too.

Why would she come to see him?

A couple of heartbeats later, she responded. "I heard."

She didn't need to elaborate, and they both knew it. Still, he hated the taut, strained feeling in the air. He wished he could do something to wipe the slate clean and put them—her—more at ease with him again.

He cleared his throat. "I appreciate your coming, especially since the last time we spent together ended on such an awkward note. I'm sorry about that, but I realize this isn't the time to go through it all again. Let's just put it aside and deal with the shelter's situation, okay?"

In the silence, he sent up a brief prayer for help, for calm and for her agreement.

But her face remained set in the stony lines it donned when he'd mentioned their earlier disagreement, and he wondered if he'd blown it again with her. The tension only grew thicker.

Then, before he had braced himself for whatever might come, she seemed to shake herself, and stepped into the office, paused at his side. Zach pushed his chair back to rise, but Gabi surprised him yet again. She placed a hand on his shoulder and gave him a gentle squeeze. "I'm so sorry."

The apprehension shot free of him in a whoosh of breath. The caring in her warm touch reached deep into that cold, blocked-off region of his heart, as she'd done before. Her presence in the shelter meant so much at that moment.

He covered her fingers with his and responded with a tentative smile. "So am I, but it's not over yet. We'll come up with something. I'm sure of that."

"I wish I could tell you I came over because I have the perfect solution for you, but I can't. I'm just here because I'd made plans to come and help Claudia with some dogs that need grooming."

"If it makes you feel any better, I don't have any brilliant answers, either."

She studied his expression. "But you said you aren't ready to give up, right?"

"Right."

"Are you still looking at it as a whole elephant, or have you started to chew on it one bite at a time yet?"

"I've only started to chew on the potential funding sources mouthful."

He saw she'd set the wheels in her head to work. "What's your greatest cost?"

Zach glanced at the statement for the rent. "The property itself. Lyndon Point gives us a reduced rate, but it's still a huge chunk of money. This is prime real estate, right in the middle of town."

She tapped her fingers on the chair's armrest in a rhythmic cadence. The tiny crevice between her brows deepened, and Zach hated to know he'd been the one to put it there, he and his troubles. He instead wished he could smooth it away with a finger, to relieve her of some of her worries. But the situation around him didn't give him that opportunity.

Not yet.

"It might sound crazy," she started, "but would you consider moving to a less expensive location?"

He blew out another explosive breath. "Wow. That would be a huge undertaking, but sure. If it was the only way to save the shelter, of course I'd do it."

"Would you mind if I talked to Aunt Edna? See what might be available?"

"I hadn't given it a thought, but it's a good idea. Go ahead, and let me know what she says."

With a deep sigh, Gabi planted her palms on the chair arms and pushed herself upright. "I can do that. Now I'd better go help Claudia. She mentioned one of the dogs might have a bad dewclaw that was never removed. It might need surgery now."

Zach rolled his eyes. "Another huge vet bill is the last thing we need."

"I know. Let's see what we can do." She smiled. "Hang in there. I'm not very good at waiting patiently for them, myself, but God's answers do come in unexpected ways and at the least expected time."

"We both know I have experience with that." Not that he'd ever wanted to gain that kind of experience. Nor did he want to have to call on it again.

It had taken all Gabi's strength to keep from arguing with Zach when she found him in his office upset about the shelter, understandable though it might be. Although she'd tried her best to be supportive, deep down she saw no point for him to smack his head against the brick wall of the town's funding problems. Why would he insist on putting himself through that nightmare when she'd tried to offer him a new future a number of days earlier?

Would it take the closing of the shelter for her to solve her problems? That never would have been her choice.

And she really did intend to help him with the shelter. She knew how much it meant to him, and if there was any way they could save it, she would do all she could. The place had found its way to a very special place in her heart, too.

Now, three days later, after her latest conversation with Aunt Edna, she was headed down to see Zach again. She wondered if the results of the Realtor's research would be of any help to him.

Claudia looked up as she walked in. "He's in the back."

"How do you know I'm here to see Zach?"

"You have a certain look on your face. It usually means there's something on your mind, and he's a part of it."

"Didn't know I was such an open book."

"I'm just the mother of five."

Gabi chuckled and made her way down the aisle of the kennel room, greeting a few of the shelter's guests as she went. "Knock, knock," she said at Zach's office door.

He pushed back from his desk, turned the chair toward her and stood. "Come in."

She plopped down on the extra chair. "Somehow I'm not surprised to see you holed up in here again."

Waves of frustration radiated from him. "It's all this money stuff. I'd much rather be out there with the animals."

"I know. But maybe what I came to tell you will help. I just talked to Aunt Edna."

He leaned toward her, a keen light in his gaze. "Did she find something we might be able to use?"

Gabi shrugged. "She found a listing that sounded promising to her and interesting to me. It's on the edge of town, to the north, just past that beach where we had the picnic."

At the thought of their romantic, sunset celebration, a warm glow swirled through her. In spite of their later disagreement, she couldn't deny the level of caring and affection it had taken on his part. It said a lot about the man in front of her.

And it meant a lot to her, too. Perhaps too much. But she'd keep the jewel-like memory in a special place, as moving as Zach's intent had been.

"Is it land or does it have a building on it already? We could never afford to have something built."

"It has a structure on it, but we don't know if it's anything that might work. It was once a gas station/body shop, and it's been empty for about four years now. From what she has learned, the owners are close to desperate to sell."

He arched a brow. "Are they desperate enough to let it go dirt cheap?"

She named a sum that made him whistle in shock. "I take it that's out of the budget."

"I suppose I could come up with it, but it means I'll have to wipe out my 401(k). I'd have to see what kind of remodeling it would need to turn it into something we could use."

His entire retirement? He was young, but that was a serious commitment. "You're that determined to do this."

He met her gaze. "I told you this was my new start."

"Do you want me to have Aunt Edna call you? You can talk to her about setting up a time to see the place."

"Sure." He paused, studying her silently. Then, "Would you want to come with us?"

Gabi's heart skipped a beat at the invitation. Deep inside she'd wanted to be a part of the solution to his dilemma, but she'd never presumed he'd want her along. Now, he'd reached out to her and, instead of doing the sensible thing and backing off, she was ready to leap forward.

With a smile on her lips, she stepped up to the pleasant if tough challenge. "I'd love to—as long as I have someone to cover for me at Tony's. I have a couple of interviews set up again."

"How's that going?"

She shrugged. "Not well. But let's not go there… unless you want us to disagree again."

"I don't want that. I seem to remember we agreed to disagree."

"I'm happy to keep it that way." For the time being.

A short while later, after they'd made plans to

work on Houdini's training again that evening, Gabi left. A woman who'd recently moved to Seattle from Atlanta was scheduled to interview for the restaurant manager position that morning, and Gabi had high hopes for this candidate.

Hopes that weren't met. The woman boasted of a long list of managerial positions at chain restaurants, but she hadn't done so much as wait on even one table in that lengthy career. Food service experience was unique, and other work didn't carry over well. Gabi's search continued.

Even though she was pretty sure she already knew the right man for the job.

Er, *jobs*.

Zach's acceptance could make the solution a two-for-one.

Chapter Eleven

"I think this may be the way to go," Zach said as he, Gabi and Edna Lyndon stepped out of the building they'd just examined. "A private operation means we'll only have to answer to the usual state and county regulations, rather than operate as an arm of the city. We'd have more leeway on our choice of location."

Gabi looked at the building with narrowed eyes, then met his gaze. "Are you sure you want to wipe out your last penny for this heap?"

He chuckled, refusing to own the touch of fear that tweaked the back of his mind. "Here I thought all women were born with the remodeling and redecorating gene. Where'd you go wrong?"

"I haven't gone wrong. I have a healthy interest in interior design, but this place looks like more than I'm ready to bite off."

The Realtor locked the front door. "You need to

use your imagination, Gabriella. And you need some courage, too. The structure is sound, the mechanicals are only about six or seven years old and the roof is a complete tear-off replacement from the summer before they closed up shop. All it needs is fresh interior drywall, chain-link kennels for the dogs, a cat section built to Zach's specifications and then a fresh, new reception area at the front."

"Don't forget the playroom," Zach added. "It's probably the most important part of the shelter. It's where the adoptions become reality."

Edna nodded. "But that's just glass installation— or do you think Plexiglas might do as good a job? I hear it's less expensive and easier to install."

"I'd have to look into it," Zach answered. "Anything reasonable that could cut costs sounds good right about now."

"What do you think about that kitchenette area in the back?" Gabi asked. "Do you think it would work for the staff room?"

"Well, guys," Edna cut in. "You can keep tossing around ideas on your own, but I'm tired, and I have an early-morning meeting. Let me know what you decide, Zach. I'll do everything possible for you."

"Thanks," he said, and meant it.

After a flurry of goodbyes, he and Gabi got back into his car, and he began the drive to her house.

"Hey," she said, casting him a sidelong glance.

"You never answered my question. What about that mini-kitchen?"

He clicked on his turn signal and made the left turn past Birdie's Nest on one corner and Ryder's wife's fabric arts store on the other. "You mentioned the staff room, but something else came to mind when I first saw it."

"A bigger bathing area for the dogs?" Gabi asked.

"Not at all. I was thinking I could build a small apartment back there for me. That way I could eliminate the cost of my own rent."

"You'd live there with all the animals?"

"Don't sound so horrified. It's not as if I'd sleep in a kennel."

She clamped her lips in a crooked line and shook her head.

Zach fought a grin. Gabi looked sweet and confused, and for some reason her expression struck him as even more appealing than any she'd worn before. Perhaps it was the ease she felt while with him. At least, he hoped that had returned.

He recognized that she would take any evidence of humor as mockery. And he knew how that had hurt her while growing up.

He never wanted to be the source of additional misery. Instead, he found himself longing to hold her and bring another smile to her lips again.

Maybe with another kiss like the one they'd shared.

He set aside his runaway imagination so it wouldn't get him into any further trouble with her.

Before she could come up with another objection, he continued. "I'd be like a caretaker. It would make it easier for me to be at work early, and I'd already be there anytime a new rescue with a health problem needed help through the night. I might wind up getting more sleep."

"I think you've lost your mind."

"Maybe. But I think I could make it work. I'd install a small bathroom that backed up against the kitchen area, since the plumbing's already in place. Shouldn't be too much work or too expensive to do."

He parked in front of the Carlini home, beautiful in the twilight. The dormers gave the house a cottage charm that made him think of postcards of the English countryside, and the flowers in the front garden on either side of the walk gave off a spicy-sweet scent that wafted in through his open window.

He waved toward the house. "Can't say I'll be living in the kind of quarters that compare to your parents' place, but I can make just about anything work. And I would hope it wouldn't be for too long."

She unclicked her seat belt and turned to face him. "I promised myself I wasn't going to bring this up again, but I can't help myself now. Blame it on my persnickety numbers and business background."

"Go ahead," he said, resigned.

"You're telling me you're going to pour your last

dime into that place to open up your own animal shelter, that you're willing to move into a back corner of the new operation—do I have it right so far?"

He had to admit, it sounded crazy when she put it that way. But he didn't see any other options. "You've got it."

"Okay, financial genius. Tell me. Where are you going to get the money to pay the lights and the water once you wipe out your last penny? How about the dog food? And what about Oscar and Claudia? Are you going to pay them in kibble?"

"The three of us have come to an agreement already, so their salaries are not an issue, at least, not for the immediate future. We're also looking into the possibility of having a dog food company or two sponsor us with food, and the utilities and everything else should be covered by the donations that come in on a regular basis."

Her skeptical expression gave him pause. Yeah, he sounded on the wrong side of crazy, but he was going to make it work. "I know I can do it."

He hoped. Not on his own, of course. God would have to do the greater part.

"Here goes, Zach. And please don't get mad. What if…" She drew a deep breath, and he saw her square her shoulders as though bracing for a battle.

Great. That wasn't the first image that popped into his mind when he thought of spending time with her. But he respected her enough to hear her out. He bobbed his head to nudge her along.

"If you do go ahead and follow through with all those plans, then what will you live on? Last time I checked, dog food's not exactly the kind of gourmet pickings you like to eat."

He shrugged. "I know I've trained my palate to prefer better things, but I can do okay with just about anything."

"You're not being realistic. How about if I draw up a business plan for you, so you can see what you really need? That way you'll know for sure you can pull it off."

No objection there. "Go ahead and draw up the business plan. It's a good idea." He took his own deep breath and plunged ahead. "But I've decided I'm going to go ahead with it."

Gabi shook her head. "I was afraid you were going to say that, so I'm going to step where I know there are more land mines than in the dogs' outside runs."

"What are you talking about?"

"You promise to hear me out? Without arguing or anything?"

He narrowed his eyes. "I'm not sure I like the sound of that, but okay. Go ahead."

"I think you need a job to support yourself if you're going to invest everything you own in a private animal shelter. Make Claudia your private shelter manager—which she already has been under your direction but without the title. Then make Oscar the head of the volunteers. Finally, load up on help from all the foster families and your team of volunteers. That's what might give you a fighting chance to make it work. But, first, you need a steady income."

He hated where he knew she was going, but he couldn't disagree with her. He knew he was taking a huge risk with this investment, one that had more than a few overtones of recklessness, but she was offering him a rope to hang on with. "I suppose you're going to offer—"

"I'm going to ask you again to do us both a favor," she said. "Please solve our joint dilemmas at the same time. You need income, and I need a chef. I need someone to run a successful restaurant, and you know how. You already have two trained employees who can manage the shelter, and while you're dealing with the remodel, you can earn a living. Make sense?"

How? How had he come to this point?

How could he possibly consider stepping into a commercial kitchen again? Hadn't he promised himself he'd never do that again? Hadn't he already failed at it once? Did he really want to risk going through that nightmare again? And this time, with someone else's restaurant? With others depending on him? An older couple, one of whom needed the income for his health? He also had to consider the woman who was putting all her trust and faith in him. How would he forgive himself if he let Gabi down?

But what else could he do? He couldn't walk away from the animals…or her.

He met Gabi's gaze. "I hate to agree with you, but it does make sense. I'll do it, though, on one condition."

"Unless it has something to do with tarantulas or piranhas, I'll take it."

Zach couldn't stop the crooked grin. "I'm not crazy about fat, fuzzy spiders, either, and toothy fish strike me as just wrong."

She laughed. "Okay. So what's this condition of yours?"

"Temporary. That's all I'm agreeing to. I'll take the job on a temporary basis. We'll talk again in… say, three months."

She cheered, then shocked him when she threw her arms around him. For a moment, a very long, enjoyable moment, they stood still, as though frozen in the warm, affectionate tone of her gesture. He slipped his arms around her and took in her smile, the sparkle of her eyes, the soft, appealing curve of her lips. He wished it could always be like this between them, and even more.

A shot of reason struck him in the heart, and he unlaced his fingers at the back of her waist. He laid his hands on her shoulders, unwilling to break the contact, no matter how much he knew he should.

Her cheeks tinted a rosy tone, and he knew without a doubt the time had come to step back. He did so with a deep sigh.

"Deal!" she said, her voice only a tad weaker than he'd grown to expect.

"Sold!" she added, this time in the stronger way he knew. "I told you I'd take whatever you were willing to offer. Temporary it is…until you see it turn into permanent. You'll see!"

Yes, they would indeed see. And he prayed God's protection over both of them. On the business end, as well as the personal one. Working together posed yet more danger than the loss of a job or even a career.

He was losing his heart to this woman.

And he didn't think he was going to do anything to stop it.

Three days later, the major changes had been set into motion. Claudia had taken over the reins at the shelter with Oscar as a willing and happy partner, and the difference in the man's attitude was a bonus. He now walked with a lighter step, and his smile reached his eyes. He looked about fifteen years younger.

At Tony's—well, Antonio's now, since it was closer to becoming a reality—Gabi had canceled all her postings for a new chef and a restaurant manager. Zach had turned in his resignation to the town council, accepted his tiny two-month salary severance and returned to the career he'd promised never to revisit.

He'd composed an ad for a sous chef, and as soon as it went up on the internet, the phone began to ring. He'd handled those interviews, and his new assistant was set to begin work the coming Monday. In the meantime, Gabi had made the rest of the choices for redecorating the dining room, and she'd devised a plan for how to accomplish the changes without causing too much disruption. After all, they couldn't afford to close down and do it all at one time.

The night before, Hannah McRoberts had helped her tile the outside of the front counter, where customers were greeted, and the glowing Italian glass tile she'd found on clearance now gave the entry a contemporary, elegant look.

Later on that night, she planned to paint the walls a coordinating soft grayed aqua, reminiscent of the ocean—in their case, the Sound. She'd already ordered a collection of prints on canvas for the walls, all of them depicting scenes of Italy but done in a contemporary style. The polished concrete floors worked well with her new vision, and the old beamed ceilings added the kind of vintage touch that benefited most designs.

She'd extracted promises of secrecy from all her

helpers, since she wasn't ready yet to let her parents see their progress.

And there was plenty left to do before they reached that point. She still had to wait for the lighting order to arrive. A handful of lantern-shaped pendants, all in polished chrome, would replace the bright red-and-green metal lampshades that had done their duty over the tables for as long as Gabi could remember. She would paint the tables themselves an enamel-black with a glossy finish, and the booths were set to be reupholstered in about a week.

The plan was for a clean, simple and sleek atmosphere so that diners could focus on the exquisite food. *Chic* was the word she kept in mind.

Gabi couldn't wait until she'd finished the transformation. In her mind, it would match the wonderful scents that were flowing from the kitchen. Zach had begun to test the recipes Gabi had found in Mama's old handwritten notebooks, and they'd agreed to taste the results of his latest efforts before the lunch crowd hit.

Lured by the promise of the delicious dishes to be tested, Gabi walked to the kitchen and paused in the doorway, admiring the newly reorganized space, not to mention the handsome man in charge. Zach had come in like a whirlwind and left her with the impression of a meticulous and picky head chef.

"What's on the menu?" she asked.

"Your mom's old family recipes are fabulous," he

answered without looking up from the stove. "I only made some minor tweaks, and they're turning out excellent. We'll be having her spinach and ricotta gnocchi, a chicken with tomatoes and shrimp, and I couldn't resist her recipe for a fresh orange granita."

"Question for you, though. How does that menu hit the budget?" she asked.

"That's the best part. Aside from the shrimp, everything is reasonably inexpensive, and only requires for the ingredients to be sourced fresh. As far as the shrimp, a few go a long way—again, as long as they're—"

"Fresh...I got it." She stepped closer and took a look at the plates. "I didn't think I was late, but you've already served the chicken and the gnocchi."

"You're just in time. Like how it looks?"

"You're right. It all looks great. But where's the granita?"

"In the freezer waiting until after the meal." He poured a thin drizzle of extra-virgin olive oil over the green and creamy white gnocchi. "So you're the kind that goes for dessert first, then?"

"Who can resist an Italian ice confection in the summer?"

He shot her that mischievous grin she'd begun to anticipate. "That's the plan for the customers."

Gabi took a moment to admire the neat orderliness of the room, the beautiful servings on the tray, the towel-draped lumps of pizza dough on the floured counter, ready to be stretched and placed on pans. Then she saw the smile on Zach's face. "You look happy," she told him. "I think you're right where you belong, and doing what God meant for you to do."

His cheerful expression vanished, and Gabi wished she hadn't been so quick to bring up the point. It could have waited until after their relaunch of the restaurant or until the cash register brimmed with their increased profits. But she hadn't been able to keep the words from slipping out, especially when they only reflected the truth.

"Don't be so quick to declare victory," he finally said, returning to the tray he'd prepared. "We haven't even served the first meal, and we don't know what the customers will think when the new dishes appear on the menu."

"I've only heard compliments on the new tile."

"That's because it's tile," he groused, discounting the impact. "It doesn't affect their taste buds or their pocketbooks. Wait until you really mess with those. The effect will be measurable then."

She gave him a wry look. "Ye of little faith. I have complete confidence that we're on the right track here, and soon you will, too."

"I guess time will tell." He picked up the tray. "Let's eat, and see what you think, boss."

Once again, Gabi sang his praises as she raved

over the food. "You really do know your way around a kitchen."

"That's never been the issue," he said, his voice quiet. "It's more a matter of the risk involved in the restaurant industry. Years of work and sacrifice were blown because of one single shipment of bad greens. And that doesn't even consider the poor people who got sick. It's not worth the risk to me."

"Look at how long my parents have been in business," she countered. "Nothing like that's ever happened to them."

"They've been lucky—blessed."

"And so will you. I can feel it."

"Maybe what you're feeling is a hankering for the granita."

She swatted him with her napkin. "That was bad, but bring on the granita. If it's as good as the meal, I can't wait."

He cleared away their dishes and quickly returned with the new cut-glass dessert cups. "Go ahead."

She picked up a spoonful and let it melt on her tongue. "Oh, yum!" She closed her eyes in appreciation. "It's so good. Sweet but tangy and wonderfully crunchy, too."

"It's too bad you don't like it," he commented with a wink.

She ignored him and had another scoop, savoring the flavor and the moment. She was having fun with him, so much fun. She wished their times together could be like this more often, but then it would make leaving that much harder to do.

Still, she wished she could stop time right then, so their easy conversation and companionship could just go on and on and on.

At least she could still relish what they shared together, so she smiled and dug into her granita with even more gusto. But before she'd had more than a third of her serving, her cell phone rang. A glance told her it was her boss, and although she was tempted to ignore the call, she didn't think she could continue to avoid him much longer.

"Hello, Damon," she said a moment later. Out of the corner of her eye, she saw Zach try to appear uninterested, but she knew he was listening to her every word.

It didn't matter. She wouldn't have anything private to say, since these phone calls always related to the job and her dwindling vacation time. With a sigh, she sat back and let Damon relate all his grievances with the business world, and, eventually, he wrapped up by telling her his tale of woe should show her how much he needed her back at her desk the next day.

"Is that all?" she asked after he fell silent.

"All?" he said with a sputter. "Everything I've told you is awful. I need you here. We can't function without you."

Gabi laughed. "That's not what I heard from some

of the others in the office. You do realize they have phones and stay in touch with me, right?"

He fell silent once again.

She went on. "I realize everyone's taken on a few of my accounts, and you have, too, but it's not like the place is falling apart. And this isn't something that's ever happened to me before. I'm not taking advantage of you. I'm doing the best I can to take care of my family." Gabi took a deep breath and twirled one of her curls around her finger. When Damon paused for breath, she forged ahead. "And I'm handling the work you asked me to do, as well. You did get the last set of files I forwarded, right? I believe I have an email from you telling me what a nice job I did."

The silence continued.

Since he didn't seem to have anything with which to counter her comments, she fell silent, too. Then, when he spoke again, he surprised her with the gruffness of his tone.

"I do understand your situation has been a tough one, and unusual, but I need you to see mine, as well," he said. "You finished the large assignment I gave you, and you did do a great job on it…."

"But…?"

"But you can't service client accounts while you're in Washington State, and the office does need a manager. I've been able to get some subs to help out, but it's not fair to the company, to your coworkers or to me for this to go on much longer. And it's not fair to you, either. If your family needs you there, Gabi, you really have to think about moving back."

He'd stunned her, and she had nothing to say.

He went on. "I need to know when...or *if*...you plan to come back. I can't keep this up much longer."

She hadn't heard Damon like this in years. She'd been afraid they would reach this point, and now they had. But she couldn't leave. Not yet. She had to make sure things were at least ready to hand over to Zach before she went back to Cleveland.

At the same time, she couldn't lose her job. "I have vacation time left, Damon. It's only right for me to take it when I need it."

"I agree. How much do you have left?"

"Thirteen business days, but I also have about a week's worth of comp time. Remember all those trips I took for you? There were a number of weekends I used to make things easier for you."

"Fair enough. That's a whole lot of time there, Gabi, and I'll give you three more weeks off to take care of your personal matters. But that's *it*. Three weeks, or you'll need to find another position."

As Damon hung up, she had to agree he'd been more than fair. Over the five years she'd worked for him, he'd let her accumulate all the unused vacation time that she'd accrued, as well as sick leave and the comp days she'd earned from working weekends. Now that her legitimate time off was nearing the end, he had the right to call her back to work.

She just hoped the restaurant would be ready by then.

As far as Mama and Papa went... Well, they'd never be ready.

And she didn't dare look up and see the expression on Zach's face. She knew what she would find there if she did.

Chapter Twelve

❧

"What do you mean, you can't take Papa to the doctor's appointment?" Gabi asked.

On the other end of the conversation, her mother's voice trembled. "Gabriella, I— No. I cannot take your Papa. Not now."

Gabi rubbed the dull ache at her brow. "But why not? You were there when he made the appointment, and knew this day was coming. Now you're running late, and you need to head down to the doctor's office right away."

A pause. "You know I don't like traffic, and it's middle of day, plus downtown's only traffic and more traffic. Please, please come with us like you have since you came home."

Oh, no. Not today. "Mama! We're having the opening with the new decor at Tony's tomorrow, and Zach and…well, everything. I still have too much to do today, so I can't leave right now to take Papa for his follow-up appointment. Besides, you're perfectly able to take him yourself."

"I—I know, but…" Mama squared her shoulders and tipped up her chin. "Bah! All that nonsense at Tony's—it's for nothing. Lyndon Point needs a pizzeria, and they have one. Fancy food's for Seattle or Edmonds or—or Queen Anne."

Ever since Gabi had let it slip that she had gone ahead and begun the overhaul of the restaurant, her mother had missed not one opportunity to oppose the entire project. At least Gabi had been able to keep her away up to now. She did want to surprise her parents, and she had sent up numerous prayers for the surprise to strike them as a good one.

Her mother's unusual silence caught Gabi's attention, worried her. Something was wrong, and her mother was hiding behind her well-known dislike of Seattle's traffic snarls. Although Mama was an anxious driver, and she did struggle whenever she was forced to confront the reality of the large city's congested roadways, she usually overcame her fear and went downtown when necessary. Especially for something as important as getting Papa to his neurologist.

"Aw, Mama. What's really wrong?"

"Oh, *figlia mia.*" Her mother's breath came out in a ragged sob. "It was so bad, that day of the stroke. I was so afraid, I didn't think your papa… I didn't think he would live. And I know we're in God's hands, but I don't want to be left alone without him."

Her mother, who'd been a pillar of strength the whole time Papa had been hospitalized, or at least she'd presented that image over the phone, now displayed anguish that stole Gabi's breath. For a moment, she couldn't say a word.

What was she going to do? She had a million things to finish at Tony's before their big day tomorrow. And yet, Mama was going through a struggle far greater than her fear of traffic. Gabi couldn't turn her back on her mother.

While she would never put it in those words, her mother's anxiety spoke volumes of her need for her daughter's company. Mama's real fear centered on the possible verdict the specialist might deliver on the pace of her father's recovery. Fear of tangling with Seattle drivers was much easier to express.

"Don't worry," Gabi said, her voice soft and full of understanding. "Papa's doing well, and you know it. The doctor's only going to have good things to say. Besides, I'll go with you. I'll hurry home so that we can go together. But let's not have any more talk about the traffic. Give me a minute, and make sure you're both ready."

She hung up, and as she turned to head to the kitchen, she crashed into Zach. "Oof!"

"That was a great thing you just did," he said.

"I know they'll be more grateful to you than you'll ever imagine."

She shrugged. "I love them. They're my parents."

"And they need you. They need you here. Remember that." As she started to argue, he continued. "You can trust me with the restaurant. So go ahead. I'll make sure everything continues to move smoothly, and I'm sure you'll be back in time to take a last look around for any detail I might have missed." He tapped the tip of her nose with a gentle finger. "If you really want to, we can argue then."

A knot formed in her throat, and she hurried to retrieve her purse from the back. By the time she made her way through the dining room again, tears had formed. Even though she tried hard not to think about it all that often, the reality of how close she'd come to losing Papa was overwhelming. What if he hadn't made it? What if, while she'd been in Cleveland, he had lost his life?

Maybe Zach had been right when he'd accused her of being self-centered. Maybe she had let her discomfort while growing up blind her to her parents' needs. Maybe that was the purpose Cleveland had served, to let her turn a blind eye to their need and distress. And maybe she'd dealt with the guilt now creeping into her heart by pushing it away, by ignoring her family's pleas for her return, by holding her relatives—yes, even Mama and Papa—at arm's length. The twinge of guilt became a growing burn, and she felt tears well up in her eyes. Blinded by the moisture, she didn't see Zach until he stopped her, his hands on her shoulders.

"Hey," he murmured. "Antonio's okay. And it's great that you can go with him to hear for yourself what the doctor has to say. Plus, you can trust me to take care of this place. Remember, I'll be here for you, waiting for you when you're done."

The gentle squeeze of his fingers made her feel a lot better. "Thanks. I'll be back as soon as I—"

"When you can. The restaurant's fine. You're doing what really matters, and you know it. Now get going before your dad really does miss his appointment."

Unwilling to acknowledge her own fears, she clamped her lips to keep them from trembling again, met his steady gaze and nodded. She had to get a grip on her emotions if she was to maneuver through the notoriously terrible traffic from the coast to downtown with any kind of success.

She couldn't help but wonder. If the news were not as positive as they all expected, would she do any better behind the wheel than her mother would have done?

As Gabi and her parents sat in the doctor's waiting room, her anxiety began to grow. What had she just done? When a conflict had come up, she'd needed Zach to step in and guide her, rescue her.

Depending on someone else was totally out of character for her. Where was her self-reliance and the self-sufficiency she'd fought so hard for?

All she needed now was for the rest of her family to jump in and start to give her advice on how to handle everything from her career, to Tony's, to Papa's medical care and her whole life in general.

Fortunately for her, the nurse came and escorted them into the exam room, putting an end to her introspection and growing alarm. Only one thought stayed with her. She had to get out of her hometown before she came to rely on Zach. She'd fought too hard to establish herself as an individual to just give up.

It didn't matter how much she'd come to care for Zach. It also didn't matter that she now knew she'd leave yet another part of her heart in Lyndon Point when she returned to Cleveland. She wasn't ready to give up her hard-won identity just yet. She'd just have to leave and deal with the ache by burying herself in her work.

As much as she chafed against Damon's ultimatum, she was glad he'd called and insisted on a firm return date. She had to get away from Lyndon Point.

And soon.

"It's so nice to see you back in town!" Shirley Wilcox exclaimed from behind her menu. The lovely lady was one of Aunt Edna's closest friends and the owner of Tea & Sympathy, a wonderful establishment that sold everything tea-related from all over the world. "I'd heard you'd done a little sprucing up in here, but this is a lot more than just a little sprucing up."

Gabi couldn't read Shirley's opinion of the changes from her half-shielded expression or her neutral tone of voice. "I hope you enjoy your meal, then. Let me know what you think. We have a wonderful new chef."

Shirley nodded, and the polished-silver Gibson-girl knot on her head bobbed gently. "Yes, and I hear he was feeding cats and dogs at the shelter right before this."

No one could miss the note of…was it sarcasm? Gabi hoped it was just plain old dry wit.

"Zach had taken a sabbatical from his true calling," she said. "He loves animals and has spent years volunteering at shelters—"

"Yes, dear. I remember all that from when they hired him."

"Oh. Well, then you know he jumped at the chance to move to our part of the country when he read about the opening at the shelter."

A sudden drop in the decibel level made her look around. She sighed, then raised her voice so that customers who'd leaned into the aisle to satisfy their curiosity could hear. "He loves it so much here that he plans to stay. Isn't it a blessing that when the town council voted to stop the shelter's funding I needed a chef? Zach stepped right up, and we're the ones who've benefited. I hope you like his take on some Carlini family recipes. As I said, he's a marvelous chef."

Sam Porter slid into the booth that backed up against Shirley's. "Ah, but does your father know everything you've done so far?" A longtime friend of Papa's, Sam owned a fancy paper-and-pen supply shop on Main Street. The two men were avid domino adversaries. "Or are you playing mouse while the big pizza-king cat's away?"

Gabi couldn't stop the blush from heating her cheeks. This was exactly what she hated most about Lyndon Point. Everyone here was either related to her or they'd known her from the time she'd worn diapers. And they all wanted to tell her how to run her life.

She took a deep breath. "Mama and Papa know I've made some tweaks here and there. We have to keep up with the times. Besides, the economy's forced us into those changes so that we can compete with eateries in Edmonds and Seattle."

"Pfft!" Myra Sorenson, Ryder's aunt on the other side of his family, piped up, as no-nonsense as ever. "Think how much trouble I'd be in if I tried to plant cacti in folks' yards when what works best in our town is the hardy stuff that withstands our gray skies and constant rain. You might want to keep that in mind, Gabriella."

Myra's landscaping business was a mainstay in town, and its recent comeback had given the outspoken woman a new platform from which to preach.

"I'll keep that in mind."

Gabi did bite back something about Myra's need of Ryder and his wife Lucie's help to keep her business from going under—his financial background was only one reason he'd been voted into office. Only recently, after the Lyndons had helped her, did Myra figure out how to put the administrative and horticultural sides of her company together. However, Gabi knew she'd only be asking for trouble if she brought up *that* particular point.

"If you will all excuse me," she said, flashing the three patrons a weak smile, "I have a number of others to greet."

The customer traffic had been a constant crush since the new and improved—in Gabi's opinion—Antonio's had opened its doors for lunch that day. Every one of them wanted to offer their input on her efforts. Because she knew her hometown, she suspected each able-bodied resident of Lyndon Point would cross the restaurant's threshold within the next twenty-four hours. The trick would be to make sure they continued to do so after the novelty of the changes wore off.

So far, the general response to the changes was mixed. She prayed for a rapid improvement.

"Hey, boss," Dylan murmured as he walked by, spiffed-up in his pressed black trousers, white dress shirt and black bowtie. "Zach wants to see you in the kitchen."

"Thanks." She turned around and fielded a smattering of greetings as she hurried to the back. She could only hope Zach was about to report the smashing success of the new menu.

She pushed through new swinging doors she'd had installed by Myra's son, who owned a construction business of some sort. "What's up?"

Without looking up from the orders he was plating, Zach said, "The good news is, those who've ordered the new dishes love them. The bad news is—"

"Can't we forget the bad news?" Her stomach tightened in knots.

"Nope. You need to know this, since we have to move on it right away." He gave her a long stare, and then went back to his prep. "We've had just as many orders for pizzas—pepperoni and Garbage Pies—as we have for the new stuff. And you didn't order pepperoni for this week. I also need someone to make pizza dough right away. Alina—" he indicated the sous chef "—and I have our hands full dealing with the more complex plates."

The dull throb at Gabi's temple kicked up its intensity again. "Is there any way you can think of for us to let customers know this is a different establishment now?"

Zach wiped his hands on the towel he'd draped over his shoulder as he strode up to her. He laid firm hands on her shoulders, and she appreciated his strength and support at a time when he'd told her something she didn't want to hear. If only...

He continued, his grasp gentle and encouraging. "It's going to take a while for them to accept that. Tony's has been part of Lyndon Point for a long time now, and you've just put it through a radical change. We need to straddle the difference, at least for the time being, if we're going to have a chance to make it all work out."

She didn't want to hear any of it, even if his understanding was evident in his warm gaze and rueful smile. She tried one more time. "But that won't fit the bistro model."

He shook his head. "The pure bistro model you've envisioned might not be the way to go. I tried to warn you. A combination of the old and the new menus, on the other hand, might do it."

When he stepped away, she felt as though her knees might wobble. Had she really reached a point where she needed his presence, his contact, to lend her strength to face an ordeal? Fear began to worm its way inside her.

She made herself focus on the matter at hand,

instead of the man a few handbreadths away. "We'll never lure customers from Seattle with a mishmash."

He yanked the towel from its perch and wiped his forehead to mask his frustration or irritation with her, or so it seemed. "So, are the ads in the *Post-Intelligencer* out yet?"

"I made sure they came out last week. I also launched the website at the same time. So far, all I've seen come in are the Lyndon Point regulars." That made her queasy. Her plan would only work if they could build on their customer base.

He glanced at the clock, then back at her, an expression of deliberate patience on his features. "It's lunchtime. Seattleites don't have time for a twenty-five-minute drive each way during their breaks. Evenings and weekends are when we might see what's going to happen."

She winced. "I confess I'm not blessed with the great gift of patience."

Grinning, he winked. "I already gathered that."

His tiny gesture and humorous comment gave her a boost she hadn't expected. Oh, my! The man was really getting to her. She smiled back. "I'm going to pretend I didn't hear you agree with me on that point."

They both chuckled.

She added, "Do you need anything other than a rush order of pepperoni?"

"All the other ingredients you've always ordered—mozzarella, provolone, sausage, the large quantities of spaghetti, ziti, lasagna. I won't refuse to serve paying customers what they want to eat—that's suicide for a restaurant." He waved toward the back storage shelving unit. "Someone needs to make another pot of your dad's sauce and more dough. We need pizzas. The kind everyone's been eating here for years."

Gabi's frustration returned with a vengeance, but she managed to tamp it down. "Okay. I'll call it all in, and I'm sure our regular supplier can get it here pretty fast, maybe even by this evening. Then I'll take over for Dylan in the dining room, since he knows how to make sauce and is better than I am with pizza dough." She shrugged. "It's probably best for me to be out there, anyway. You know, to field questions or complaints. I'm sure those will come sooner or later."

His expression softened again, and his voice grew gentle. "Be prepared."

With a nod and a sigh, she went back out to the busy dining room. Even the soothing classical music overhead did nothing to mute the loud hubbub, as loud as it ever had been. The contrast between the noise and the new elegant gray-and-aqua decor jarred the senses.

Would any of the changes she'd considered crucial even be possible to achieve? She hated to agree with Zach on the point, but she suspected he might be right. "Oh, help me, Lord."

By Wednesday, however, the phone had begun to ring. Zach had been proved right on at least one point. The ads Gabi had placed, along with the internet presence, had made people from Seattle, Lynnwood and other nearby towns take notice. A fair number were willing to give Antonio's a try over the weekend and had gone ahead to make reservations.

On the other hand, since they'd instituted the change, she'd noticed a drop among Lyndon Point residents for the evening meal. The fancier menus she'd had printed listed no pizzas, no plain spaghetti and meatballs, no chopped romaine salad and no children's selections.

By then, Gabi feared Zach had been right on that point, too. And she couldn't afford to lose those patrons. She needed to build on Tony's base, not start from scratch. They could never afford that.

Her anxiety intensified during the first weekend, as the pattern continued. Still, reservations for midweek evenings and the next weekend stayed steady. Traffic on the website also increased. Evidently, the first new diners seemed to be a-buzz over their experience, and they'd spread the word. The print ads weren't hurting, either.

She and Zach established a smooth work rhythm that now ran like a fine-geared European sports car.

A nod of his head, a particular look from her to him, quickly accomplished the desired result. After that first day, they came up with a master food list to accommodate the old Tony's standards for the lunch crowd, and Gabi continually adjusted it to account for the increasing need of more upscale ingredients for the evening meals.

Their easy partnership worked great for the restaurant. However, it scared the daylights out of her on the personal front.

She was already too involved with Zach. Their work at the restaurant only deepened their relationship. And they had shared that kiss. A kiss that invaded her dreams night after night and one that she secretly yearned to experience again.

She couldn't let her feelings for him grow any deeper. But the longer she continued to work so closely with him, which included training Houdini together in their free time, the greater the danger. She had to leave Lyndon Point again. Before she changed her mind and stayed.

For good.

There were no two ways about it—life in Lyndon Point put her independence at risk. Not only did her large family live here, ready to swoop in and take over at any moment, but the relationship with Zach also put her at risk of losing herself. Her mother's fear of having to live on without Papa was only the latest example of the kind of need, of dependence she didn't want. Gabi longed for the self-sufficiency she'd gained by forging a life of her own far from her family's center of gravity.

But before she could go back to Cleveland, Antonio's had to be on the road to success. The concept so consumed her that it almost took over her every thought, practically at all times.

"Hey!" Hannah cried from across the table at lunch the next day. "Sharing a meal with a zombie that looks like Gabi Carlini is not what I had in mind."

"I'm sorry. I just have a lot on my mind."

Her old high school chum grinned. "I'd say. He's about six feet tall, and looks better in an apron than anyone else I've seen."

At the mention of Zach, she glanced toward him as he stood in the kitchen doorway, leaning against the door frame. The white uniform jacket emphasized the width of his shoulders, and set off his tan to perfection. Hmm… Hannah did have a point. How a big guy like him could look so good in these surroundings escaped her. Gabi just knew he did.

As she studied him, she saw the mischievous grin spread across his lips. She met his gaze, and stared, a sense of private knowledge flying between them. That kiss…

She tried to fight the blush but knew it was a losing battle. "Aw, come on. I'm in danger of losing my job if I don't go back, Mama's scared of losing

Papa, as am I, and I need to make sure the changes I've made here pay off. I don't have time to notice anyone's apron."

"Your red face says otherwise." As Gabi sputtered, Hannah's expression turned thoughtful. "You know," she began, "life doesn't always revolve around a high-powered career. Dollars and titles and accomplishments of that kind are nice, but they won't be there for you when you need a warm embrace and a hand holding yours. You could build a full, satisfying life here in Lyndon Point, surrounded by all those who love you. And I'm sure you wouldn't be opposed to the 2.5 kiddos and a dog or so."

Stunned by Hannah's words, Gabi could only gape.

Her friend, however, wasn't done yet. She glanced at Zach again, and the two women watched him slip back inside the kitchen.

Hannah chuckled. "I doubt he'd oppose anything I've mentioned, either. I saw the way he looked at you. Seems like there's something there, after all. You might want to think about it."

Cheeks aflame, Gabi chose to ignore her friend. "What are people saying about the new menu?"

Hannah's gaze hit the tabletop, and she twisted the corner of her linen napkin. "Um…well, they say the food tastes good."

"That's not a ringing endorsement."

"It's just that it's…*different*."

"Do you think it's a matter of time?"

Hannah fixed her blue eyes on Gabi, and she felt the stare as though her friend was reaching inward to her buried fears. "I think they're having to make a choice, and it's not one they want to make. Tony's has always meant pizza and spaghetti, the easy, cozy and familiar. They could also afford it on a regular basis. Antonio's, on the other hand…"

"But we still do the pizzas. Zach has insisted on putting them back on the lunch menu."

"That's the point, Gabi. The regular things are only on the lunch menu. Evenings, people are heading over to the Nest. Many of them don't have the extra cash these days to plunk down for the specialty dishes, no matter how good they are—a chicken breast in a fancy sauce is more expensive than a slice of pizza and a soda. Imagine what it means when you have to feed a family."

"So I'm going to need Seattle customers instead of those from Lyndon Point to increase profits."

Hannah looked sad. "And say goodbye to Tony's."

That hit Gabi hard. She hadn't thought of it that way, not in that final sense. She was only upscaling the restaurant, not putting an end to it. Right?

"It's not goodbye to Tony's," she argued. "Tony's is Antonio's. The only difference is that one is more elegant and upscale, more twenty-first century than the other."

"It won't ever be the same."

But would it be better?

Time to switch gears. "Help me out here, Hannah. What do you think would be the best way for me to draw more of the foodie crowd from Seattle?"

"Ha! You're asking me? I just finished telling you about the pizza crowd. Didn't you hear me?"

"I heard you. It's just that you have a good head on your shoulders, and you told me you spent years working downtown at that high-powered insurance company's executive offices."

Hannah thought for a moment. "You've hit the *Post-Intelligencer,* right?" At Gabi's nod, she went on. "How about the local-interest magazines? The internet?"

"Yes and yes."

"Okay, so…foodies. They do like to shop at the Pike Place Market, but that's not going to work. How about all those ritzy gourmet shops in Bellevue and the more funky ones in Fremont? Have you sent out mailers to any of them?"

"I hadn't thought of it, but I can do that. Sounds like a good possibility—"

"Oh!" Hannah opened her eyes wide. "I've got it. All of them follow the decrees of the food critics to a T. They're always talking about the latest restaurant reviews and recommending those places to each other. Have you invited any—"

"Critics!" She grinned back. "You're brilliant. I

haven't, but I really should. Why didn't I think of it before?"

Hannah winked. "You're the one who said it. I'm *brilliant*."

"I'll give you that one. Of course, I'm going to do it, right away, before I even go to bed tonight. But don't tell anyone, okay? If it doesn't pan out, I don't want anyone to know a critic didn't think we were good enough for their snooty palate to review."

"Sure. I don't have a problem with that. My lips are sealed."

While they finished eating, Gabi's thoughts bounced between the conversation and the letter she was mentally composing for any and all critics within a fifty-mile radius of Lyndon Point. At least one of them would bite.

She hoped.

Hannah was right. That was exactly what they needed—a great review from a restaurant critic. She couldn't wait to surprise Zach with the news after she had it all set up. Or maybe she wouldn't tell him until after the review was published. She didn't want to disappoint him if none of it panned out.

Chapter Thirteen

"Let's work with Houdini on the fetch exercise again," Zach suggested as they closed the restaurant the next Thursday night. "I know it's late, but this won't take long, maybe fifteen minutes, since his attention span is about as long as a sneeze. We have to make sure we reinforce what we've taught him on a regular basis, or we'll have to start from square one every time we try to work with him. It's a matter of repetition."

Gabi chuckled. "You mean we'd wind up doing something like that old groundhog movie?"

"Exactly."

She turned off the kitchen lights, and they crossed through the dining room to the front door. "Oh, I don't know. I think Houdini's got us all figured out. He's aware we're the keepers of the treats, and he'll do whatever we ask of him, as long as we keep them coming. He does love to eat."

"That's because he's a terrier, and they're notoriously food motivated." He stepped to the street side of the sidewalk as they headed toward the Carlini home, and Gabi smiled at the old-fashioned, gentlemanly gesture.

"Thanks," she said.

He shrugged and smiled. "Mom had rules, and they've stuck with me all these years."

"You miss her." It wasn't a question.

"Both of my parents." He sent her a sideways glance. "Enjoy yours. They won't always be here."

A sharp pang struck.

"I don't think I'm ready to deal with that possibility."

"You never are," he said, shaking his head. "I know I wasn't, even though they'd been ill for a while. I suppose you never are, especially if you have to face another loss shortly after they're gone."

"Your restaurant..."

"Mmm-hmm. I don't know if I'd have been ready to deal with that, but that soon after their deaths I was still raw inside. Facing failure is never easy, but facing it alone is devastating. I don't wish that on anyone."

A chill ran through Gabi. "Then you can understand why I'm not ready to even think about losing either one of them."

He reached out and took her hand. Her breath caught in her throat for a moment, but her fingers curled into his without a conscious thought. When she realized what she'd done, she settled back and enjoyed the moment, the shared confidences, the companionship that felt so, so right.

His presence in her life felt right. But she wasn't ready to deal with that, either. She let the silence lengthen between them and he didn't try to break it. They walked in the comfortable hush of night, their steps illuminated by the clear glow of moonlight. It was yet another precious moment at Zach's side.

After a while, he brought up the terrier again. They went over their plans for Houdini's training, and Zach told Gabi he wanted to arrange for Houdini to be walked past the elementary school while kids played outside during recess when classes started in the fall. For the rest of the summer, the playground at the beach park on the south end of town would do. He thought one of Claudia's kids would appreciate earning a couple of extra dollars from walking the dog.

"Sure, but why the beach park?" she asked. "Houdini can't play with the kids at the park. There are signs all over saying no dogs are allowed there. That doesn't sound like the socializing you told me he needed. At school it'll be the same thing. Kids have to stay inside the perimeter fence."

"That *is* what we want. It's great he's so friendly, but therapy dogs go into hospitals, and for safety reasons they have to do what they're told. They can't run toward the first kiddo they see there, even if he's leashed. A leash can catch someone unexpectedly."

"Well, I still have a hard time believing he'll listen when there's a potential playmate on the other side of a chain-link fence, but I suppose we can see how it goes," she said, looking less than convinced that the training would work.

By then, they'd reached the Carlini home. They played with the dog for a few minutes to help him burn off his initial excitement. Then they worked with him, and Houdini's antics kept them laughing the whole time.

Gabi wished their days could be like this, full of warmth and shared happiness. She wished for an ever-lengthening time with Zach at her side.

If only…

What a great evening! And the best part about it? Zach had a great time with her, and he could tell she enjoyed his company, too. When they finished and went to put away the toys and treats, Zach had to fight the urge to kiss Gabi again. He just couldn't let himself fall any more in—

Whoa! That was a dangerous thought. He had to get away from her before he did something crazy and got himself in any deeper. "I'll see you first thing tomorrow," he said at the front door. "It's Friday. Are you ready for the rush?"

She grinned. "Weekend rush means a full cash register. I can handle that."

He stared down into her beautiful brown eyes. Oh, yes. He wanted to kiss her, but if he did, it could get awkward the next morning, since they'd be the only ones at the restaurant for a while. He didn't need that, neither one of them did. He had to focus on the day's menu, and Gabi had a way of taking over his thoughts. Another kiss would surely make things worse. In the end, he only said, "Good night."

In the morning, as he started prepping for the day, a sense of satisfaction he hadn't experienced since Gabi had walked into the shelter and turned his life upside down came and caught him by surprise. Then, after he'd quit his job at the shelter to join her at the restaurant, he'd been too afraid he could put the Carlinis' restaurant at risk, and with it their future. He hadn't been able to enjoy the work itself.

But Zach could now recognize how well the transition had gone, much better than he'd expected. And he did enjoy the shared sense of accomplishment he got from working with Gabi. He'd also come to accept that, no matter how bad his last experience had been, the culinary arts still captured his imagination in ways no other work could.

Maybe he would go back to cooking again. At least, he was pretty sure he could do it this way, by only focusing on the food itself and making sure he helped Gabi increase the restaurant's profits. The last thing he wanted was the threat of a restaurant critic's bad review hanging over his head again. As a chef, he'd lived by the latest write-up; those same write-ups had killed his restaurant in the end.

He had to get his head clear on this whole thing. He wanted to help Gabi, and he knew he had the skill to do it, but at the same time, he didn't want her family's future to hinge on those same skills. They'd failed him once before. Perhaps not so much his cooking ability, but his judgment in choosing produce providers had proved faulty, with disastrous results. He couldn't let that happen again.

And, yes. He wanted nothing to do with the brutal judgments of those who'd set themselves up as experts on food. He preferred to be judged by the regular customers who came to eat simply for the pleasure to be gained from the experience.

The reviews still stung, and maybe he should be past all that. Still, the critics had savaged him, even though they'd known the load of produce that sickened his restaurant's patrons had not been the only tainted batch shipped from the producer. Additional orders from a new organic farmer had appeared in various parts of the country. Zach was called negligent because he'd given a chance to someone other than the latest darling of a segment of the Sacramento foodie crowd.

He'd tried to do the right thing. He'd paid doctors' bills and emergency room visits. He'd dealt with his insurance company when they'd increased his rates to an exorbitant level, and through the whole ordeal, he'd been foolish enough to give the media a number of interviews.

With that kind of exposure, critics had come to his restaurant from every foodie corner without announcing their presence. They'd panned his food. They'd also taken a great deal of glee in his misery and told the story of the tainted produce in every bad review they wrote, implying he'd been negligent in his choice of organic supplier.

The experience had soured him on critics and convinced him he wanted nothing more to do with the industry. But he still loved to cook.

And he loved working with Gabi. Yes, he did have it bad for her. He couldn't say with certainty he'd fallen in love, but he suspected he might be more than halfway there.

If only she weren't so determined to go back to Cleveland, then he might pursue the attraction between them and see where it would take them. They had a lot in common, not the least of which was their faith. If it hadn't been for his assurance of God's goodness, he never would have made it through the rotten days after the salmonella incident.

He knew that after she left, he'd have to turn to his Heavenly Father again. And yet, his faith was one based on hope. Maybe they had been brought together for more than just one reason. Maybe there was more to their partnership than just friendship and desire to improve her parents' restaurant.

But, no. He couldn't let himself think about any of those dangerous maybes. She'd made her position clear from the start, and he had no interest in Cleveland. Besides, he was using every bit of his 401(k) to buy the former gas station on the edge of town. He'd asked for and received bids for the new animal shelter, and he'd presented them, together with the purchase contract, to the mortgage company. Now, he had to wait until they came back with their decision on the financing.

He couldn't afford to move to Cleveland even if he wanted to.

At the same time, he couldn't get rid of the niggling sense at the back of his mind that Gabi would make a mistake if she went back east. Something told him she belonged in Lyndon Point just as much as he did.

"Yeah, Gabi," he muttered to himself. "Maybe— just maybe—it's that terrific family of yours that makes me so certain. Or maybe it's your father's still-shaky health…and the reality that while your parents aren't elderly, they aren't growing younger? And how about the fact that *I'm* in Lyndon Point and wouldn't mind seeing where our feelings might lead?"

Oh, yeah. Sarcasm and a private rant would

get him far. And he was really objective about it, wasn't he?

"Hey!" Gabi yelled right behind him.

He nearly jumped about a foot off the ground, and the knife he'd been using clattered into the steel sink. Swinging around to face her, he frowned. "Why'd you do that?"

"I've only been standing here, trying to talk to you for the past two minutes while you muttered something to yourself. Are you okay?"

No, he wasn't okay. Especially not if she'd heard any of what he'd just said. He stole a look at her, but she didn't appear as though she had.

What she had done, though, was invade his thoughts—and even dreams—from almost the first moment they met. Now, nearly a month later, he was having a hard time evicting her from his heart. But he couldn't tell her that.

"Yes, I'm fine. Or, I will be, as soon as my pulse returns to normal."

She rolled her eyes. "Speaking of fine, I just had a call from Meghan. She's not fine yet. She won't make it in to work today, says that bug she came down with day before yesterday's still getting the best of her."

"What about Kirstie?"

"She worked the day before, then filled in for Meghan yesterday. I'll see if she's available again, but she usually volunteers at the assisted-living facility on her days off, and it's hard to catch her at the last minute."

"What about the other server you hired day before yesterday? Do you think that one could start today instead of Monday?"

"He said he wouldn't be able to start until Monday, since he's scheduled to work at his old job through tomorrow."

"Well, then, let's hope Kirstie can come in. Otherwise, can you handle the dining room alone with Dylan?"

"I think so, but it'll make for a crazy day. I'll just have to run between the tables and the register. If worse comes to worst, I'll call Mama. But that means Papa will have to come, too, since we can't leave him alone yet. He still needs help to use the restroom and even to get a glass of water."

"Hopefully it won't come to that, unless we're really, really stuck." He couldn't think of anything else they could do. "Unfortunately, I can't spare Alina. She won't be here for an hour, but I was planning to ask her to come in to work earlier starting Monday. There's really more to do back here than what the two of us can cover easily."

She sighed. "I knew we were shorthanded before Meghan called in sick. Let's hope we can have a smooth day in spite of all that."

"And the evening, too. Don't forget…it's Friday."

"Is this going to be one of those 'be careful what

you wish for' things? I wanted more customers, but today might be a good day for the old normal."

"We'll see."

She hesitated, worry etching a line across her smooth forehead. More than anything, he wanted to comfort her. To tell her that everything was going to be okay. He was about to offer a silent prayer, but from somewhere deep inside he pulled up the courage to say, "How about we pray about it? We can't go wrong by asking for God's help."

Her smile came slowly, but it did grow wide and warm. "I'm in." She reached out to him. "We always hold hands when we pray together in our family."

He curled his fingers around hers and called on their Lord. "Father, we never know what You have planned for each day, but we do know Meghan could use a touch of Your healing love right now. And we're left to turn to You and trust. Help us do our best for the customers who walk in, even if we're not at full strength. Thank You for blessing us with Your daily provision…. Amen."

Gabi walked back into the kitchen a few minutes after they'd finished praying. "Zach," she said, her voice little more than a whisper. "Remember when I said that Kirstie was planning to go to the assisted-living facility today? Well, she had to cancel. Turns out she came down with the sneezing and hacking thing, too."

He let out a breath. "Okay. That's not good, but we'd already decided if it came to it, you and Dylan would handle the dining room. Let's see how it goes before we call your mother."

Gabi's stomach lurched and she wished she were still in bed, the morning nothing more than a nightmare. "Worse has come to worst, and that plan won't work. I just talked to Dylan, too. He's—"

"No! Not him. He can't be sick, too."

She shut her eyes tight, wishing it would all just go away. "It kills me to say it, but he *is* sick. He's running a fever, and his dad's giving him a ride to the doctor as soon as the office opens."

The way Zach closed his eyes, as though he was in pain, only made her feel worse. She wanted to say something, do something to make things work again, but she was flat out of ideas.

"Now, wait," Zach said. "Something's wrong here. Are you sure they're not pulling some crazy joke on us or something? They can't all be sick at the same time."

"Trust me, I asked, but they're all miserable. Turns out this virus broke out at the assisted-living facility, and Kirstie probably picked it up there. Two of the senior citizens are in serious condition, and were even rushed to the hospital."

"That's awful."

"It really is. Meghan must have picked it up from Kirstie, since the two of them are best friends. They spend practically every minute together. Then they both work with Dylan—"

"Waiting tables is thirsty work, and I've heard them ask what cup belongs to whom."

"I'm sure they've mixed them up more than once."

They fell silent, and the only sound in the kitchen came from the ticking clock on the wall.

Zach's phone rang at the same time the motion sensor on the front door beeped. *It's Edna,* he mouthed.

Gabi left him to his call, her thoughts full of worry.

"Hi, Gabi." Alina's smile faded as Gabi approached. "What's wrong? Is your father—"

"Papa's fine." She swallowed hard. "It's our wait staff that's not." Briefly, she explained about Meghan, Kirstie and Dylan calling in sick.

Alina shook her head. "It's not just the three of them. What they have is a nasty summer cold thing that seems to have started at the assisted-living facility and the day care center. My husband's at home with Tyler, waiting for my mom to get there so she can watch him for us. My poor little guy's had it for the past three days. A lot of people in town have it. Maybe we won't have as many customers today."

"Maybe not for lunch, but I just checked the reservations calendar. We're booked pretty solid. I don't want to call those people and cancel their plans unless I absolutely have to."

"I would offer to help, but—"

"You and Zach have your hands full in the kitchen. But with your son sick, just make sure you wear one of the masks in the box on the second shelf of the pantry. I'll have to keep thinking, to come up with something. Don't worry, I'll work it out."

Alina walked away, and Gabi began to panic. Three days earlier, she'd gotten that one call she'd been hoping for. The much-respected critic for a Seattle gourmet weekly had phoned to introduce herself. She wanted to review the restaurant and wanted to make a reservation three weeks in advance. Gabi hadn't wanted to put it off that long, and she'd persuaded the woman to come in for an early dinner… on Friday. That Friday. At five-thirty—only nine and a half hours away.

Her impatience had bit her in the nose again.

Now, after cajoling the woman into using her only free evening in weeks on Antonio's, Gabi couldn't see how she could call and cancel. Maybe she could pull it off if she could get Mama to come in with Papa at around a quarter to five. Her parents would only have to stay at the restaurant an hour and a half at the longest.

That wasn't the kind of surprise she wanted to spring on Zach. Not on a day like today.

She grabbed her phone and called home. To her surprise, a woman other than her mother answered. "Who is this?" Gabi asked.

"I'm sorry. This is Shirley Wilcox speaking. The Carlinis are not available. May I help you?"

"Shirley, it's Gabi! What's wrong? What happened to Papa?"

"Nothing's happened to your father. It's your mother. I called to remind her of our plans for this afternoon. We'd made plans to take your father to an afternoon matinee of that new spy thriller he's been talking about for a while now, but she was coughing so bad she could hardly talk."

"Mama's sick?"

"Half the town's down with it," Shirley said. "Last time this happened was about five years ago, right after you started that job of yours in Cleveland. The town has so many activities in the month of June that everyone's out spreading their germs all over the place."

"But—but flu season's in the fall and winter."

"It's not flu," Shirley said. "It's a cold, but it's a bad one. I'm here to keep your parents company for part of the day, so your mother doesn't have to get close to your father. So far, he doesn't seem to have caught it, and we want to keep it that way."

Guilt hit Gabi. She hadn't even thought about that. "Thanks. I'm sure Mama and Papa appreciate your help. I know I do. It's very kind of you, but aren't you afraid you'll catch it next?"

"Think nothing of it, honey. Besides, I had it last week, and I'm afraid that may be where your mother caught it. Angela Logan's had it, too, and she'll take over for me this afternoon."

While her mother and Shirley seemed to have the situation under control at home, things at the restaurant looked worse by the minute. Maybe Gabi should just pull up her big-girl pants, call the critic and cancel. Postponing would be better than giving the woman poor service and risking a bad review. The thought of the conversation made her sick—

No! Not sick. There was enough sickness going around already.

The motion sensor beeped again. Gabi looked up as Lucie Lyndon and Hannah walked in, both in matching black trousers and white dress shirts. "Put us to work," her old friend said. "We drew morning duty."

"Morning duty?"

"Edna called a little while ago," Lucie said. "She said Shirley had asked if she would spend the evening with your parents, after Angela went home, since your mom's sick. She wanted to ask if we want to lend you a hand until your servers are better. So we're here. Show us the ropes."

"Are you kidding me?" Gabi asked.

"Not at all," Lucie answered, chuckling. "You know Edna. By now, she probably has your whole family and a bunch of friends scheduled to come in and help out. She said she was going to drive in to Seattle and pick up a stash of bow ties for everyone." She gestured at her clothes. "Edna was sure anyone could find a pair of black pants and a white shirt to wear."

This time, Gabi really had gone down Alice's rabbit hole. "Oh, my poor head. I need coffee."

Hannah headed toward the kitchen. "Tell me the ratio, and I'll start it. I may sound crazy, but, I feel the weirdest kind of guilty pleasure. My husband's taking care of the twins by himself while I'm here. I can't wait to see how that goes."

Gabi sat in the nearest chair. "This is nuts! Why are you guys doing this? You don't have to. I'm sure I can figure out what to do.... I can call a temp agency if it comes to that."

"I'm sure you can." Lucie wiggled her fingers in the air. "But we have willing hands. Now that I married your cousin, I consider myself part of the family. As it turns out, your family wants to help, especially after your father's stroke. So do you use the nice linen napkins for lunch or do you keep those for dinner? I can start setting tables."

As Gabi forced herself out of her frozen state, the door opened again. To her dismay, her aunt Sophia, one of Mama's cousins, marched right in. "Gabriella! I've not seen you since you graduated, *ragazza*. Give me a hug, and then I can help that young man of yours. Marianna says he's a beautiful one who cooks like he came from Italy himself. I can peel onions and garlic for him."

"Uh…hi. Um, Zach's done fine since he started working here, *Zia* Sophia. We can handle this. I don't think he needs…"

By then, she was talking to her aunt's retreating back. She groaned. This was her worst nightmare. Her family had arrived.

"Hey," Lucie said, and laid a soft hand on Gabi's shoulder. "She's only here for a little while. You may see a lot of your relatives for the next couple of days, but everyone agrees you still call the shots, and I doubt your customers will realize what's going on. All we want to do is help. Tell us what you need."

She nodded as though in a haze, then turned to her friend. "But, Hannah, you said no one in town was crazy about the changes. I was pretty sure they wouldn't be. Why do they want to help?"

Hannah looked stunned. "Are you serious? You don't know?"

She shook her head.

"Well, I'm not going to tell you. You're just going to have to watch and figure it out. It's not an explanation kind of thing. It's a family kind of thing—and friends, too."

Hannah slapped the swinging doors, presumably on her way to the commercial coffee urn. Lucie reached into the tall cabinet at the right-hand corner of the dining room and rummaged inside until she found the napkins.

Gabi followed the promise of coffee to the kitchen,

where she found Zia Sophia wrapped in an apron, putting together a kettle of sauce.

"I can't tell you how grateful I am she showed up," Zach murmured as she walked past. "She's taking over the sauce and the dough so Alina and I can finish our prep and get things going for the lunch crowd."

"I'm so happy to help you and Marianna and Antonio," Sophia said, her face serious. "It's good for him to stay home, and Marianna has to get over the cold."

As the day went by, a cousin here and a neighbor there came to help, each one wearing the black pants and white shirts. Aunt Edna's bow ties did the trick, as well.

To Gabi's relief, her fears of a circus atmosphere never materialized. Neither did her relatives' nosy or bossy attitudes. After she pushed past her initial shock and dismay, she realized how well-intentioned everyone was. Almost without thought, she went into career placement specialist mode and assigned jobs according to what she thought were the person's abilities. She made sure every job at Antonio's was covered.

She had the aunts making Tony's original menu items, especially the sauce, meatballs and regular lasagna. The cousins, many of whom had put in time at the restaurant before moving on to jobs they were better suited for, waited on tables as though they'd never stopped, and two uncles-a-couple-of-times-removed called to offer Zach help with cleanup after the last customer left. Although she never would have expected it, she kept everything running smoothly, and, aside from resounding greetings from Tony's regular customers, nothing seemed any different than any other day.

Still, as the clock moved closer to the five-o'clock mark, Gabi's nerves grew tighter than Zach's shelter funding. The critic was due any minute, and she didn't know what to expect. Finally, after she dropped a coffee mug in the kitchen, Zach grabbed her by the arm and walked her out the back door.

"Okay," he said, his gaze serious and worry evident in his every feature. "I know today's been crazy, but nothing's really gone wrong—except the things you dropped, the customer orders you mixed up and now the coffee you spilled. What's wrong?"

Her nerves snapped, and as though she'd been the kitchen faucet and he'd just turned the handle, her tears poured.

Chapter Fourteen

"You did *what?*" Zach asked a minute later, his eyes narrowing.

"I wanted to surprise you, and I arranged for a critic to come and review the restaurant. Her reservation's for five-thirty, and I'm so nervous I can't stand myself any longer. What if I drop her water on her? What if one of our replacement wait staff brings her the wrong meal? Oh, I just want this to go well for the restaurant and for you—"

"For me?" His voice rang with the horror splayed across his face. "What made you think I'd ever want another critic anywhere near me again?"

She froze. "But I thought they really mattered to chefs."

"They matter because they can ruin you. Who do you think put the final nail in my restaurant's coffin?"

"What do you mean?"

"I told you about the scandal after those people

who ate at my restaurant wound up sick from eating food I made. How do you think the scandal became a scandal?"

"Reporters?" she said in a weak voice.

"They reported the outbreak of salmonella, but it was the restaurant critics who kept the story going even after everyone recovered. They were the ones who played on people's fears. And they were the ones who painted me as negligent in my choice of supplier."

"Why would they write about that? Or about you? I thought they just talked about whether the food and the restaurant service were good or bad."

"They write about anything related to the restaurants they visit, including the owners and chefs. Bad greens were part of the story for a couple of days, but then the critics took it upon themselves to broadcast every last exaggerated detail of my disaster. They also seemed to enjoy writing about me and what they called my arrogance, because I chose a new start-up organic farmer instead of their preferred, sanctioned few."

She went ice-cold. "I didn't know. I know business, and I know Tony's, but what you're saying is that the upscale restaurant circles are unfamiliar territory to me, even after I did tons of research."

"Research is no substitute for experience."

"Evidently."

He rubbed his forehead, and she was sure he now

had a headache. "When did you say she was supposed to show up?"

"She made a reservation for five-thirty today, but she hadn't shown up when I went to the kitchen for that cup of coffee I dropped." She pulled out her cell phone and grimaced. "It's almost six o'clock now."

"Don't worry about the exact time," he said, his face belying his words. "She won't show up at five-thirty. That's just a heads-up she's given you. She'll show up sometime today, but she won't identify herself, so you won't know when she's here. She might even be gone by now."

"*What?* But how will we know who she is?"

"That's the whole point. She doesn't want us to know. She's been kind enough to let us know she's coming today, but the rest is up to us. We have to do our best with everyone. That's one of the things she'll evaluate."

"I thought those were mystery shoppers who did that."

"Some reviewers, the more famous ones, can't hide and so they let you know when they're coming. The same thing goes with the rating services when you're shooting for more stars. But some reviewers from smaller gourmet publications prefer to judge everything for themselves, including the overall experience. They don't want preferential treatment, since they feel regular customers won't attract the kind of attention a reviewer would."

"Oh, no."

"Yeah. Oh, no."

Now she was the one rubbing her forehead. "And on the day our regulars are out."

"Exactly." He tightened his jaw. "I told you I never again wanted to put myself through the nightmare that destroyed my dream once before. I can't believe you went behind my back and did this. If they rake up my past they could really destroy me—and take Antonio's down with me."

He yanked open the kitchen door and stormed back inside.

What had she done?

Not only had she done the one thing that was sure to cause him the most hurt, but she'd also let her pride get the better of her. She'd been so sure of her choices when it came to the restaurant that she might have done the single thing certain to bring it down.

And with it, her parents' future.

On top of that, she'd opened herself to a kind of public scrutiny she'd never experienced before. From what Zach had just said, the restaurant critic was free to examine her choices, her taste, her efforts and, yes, her failure.

It was happening on the day when her greatest weakness had become most glaringly visible. Gabi cringed at the thought of being featured in a review that could reveal how she'd needed her large family to step in and turn around her failure to properly staff the restaurant.

And she *had* failed. What kind of career placement specialist, the manager of the flagship office at one of the country's leading staffing enterprises, failed to line up enough staff to handle unexpected contingencies? What kind of business executive needed her rambunctious family to ride in, in a moment of crisis, to save her skin?

At this time when she'd most wanted to show herself capable, she found herself feeling like the neediest member of her family, like a child who couldn't stand alone. Where had the strong, independent individual who'd worked so hard to become a success gone?

Or had she ever existed in the first place?

Gabi couldn't believe she'd tumbled right back into the old patterns, into her old identity, into the trap Lyndon Point had always been for her. And it was going to be splashed all over some snooty magazine for everyone to read.

As sick to her stomach as the whole mess she'd created made her feel, she knew she couldn't run and hide. She had to get back inside the restaurant and do her best to keep it all from going to ruin. She'd have plenty of time later to lick her wounds.

Much later.

She stood and stared up toward the heavens. "Okay, Lord. I may have let my pride and arrogance convince me I know better than everyone else, and I may have hurt Zach." She took a step back and slumped down onto the top step. "Well, I know I did—and exposed him to more embarrassment than he'd already gone through. And okay, I went against what I knew Mama, Papa and the rest of the family would have wanted for Tony's."

She sat in silence as it all sank in. Part of her wanted to start running and not stop until she slammed the door of the little cottage in Cleveland behind her, but she knew she couldn't do that. She hadn't fallen that far yet. "But I did make a mess of things, didn't I? It's hard to admit, but I may have just destroyed any shred of trust Zach might have had in me. And that hurts. He matters to me. A lot."

She studied her hands for a silent, thoughtful moment. "It's time for me to face the truth, Father. I—I do...*care* for him." She sighed. "Okay, okay. Truth time, right? I'm falling in love with him, and even though it's not the wisest thing I've ever done, it's also not the craziest or most foolish. He's a good man, and I've hurt him. Father, I need the chance to apologize to him, ask his forgiveness...as I'm doing Yours now."

A tear rolled down her cheek. How could she have made such a mess of things? They'd been in chaos to begin with, and it seemed she'd only made matters worse. Still, she remembered a teaching by her pastor back in Cleveland. Reverend Troyer had said that God could redeem anything, even the wrongs His children made. He could, as long as the way-ward child surrendered to His greater wisdom and followed His Word more closely every day.

She drew a shaky breath. "At least, I don't have to give up yet, right? There must be something I can do to keep things from getting worse." She caught herself. "There must be something You could have me do, something to repair, to restore what I've ruined. Show me, Lord. Please!"

God, in His ultimate wisdom, didn't see fit to send her a flash of inspiration. Instead, a quiet certainty grew insistent in her conscience. "At least I confessed, right? That has to count for something. And I do ask Your forgiveness, Father."

She shook her head, horrified by how far she'd let things go. The first step to take if she was going to make things better was to go back into the restaurant and face the mess she'd made. She had a lot of forgiveness to ask from a lot of people, but at least she'd started out by facing God.

With a heavy heart and heavier steps, she went back inside to the reality of what she'd done. Yet, aside from Zach's obvious stress and his clenched jaw, nothing seemed to have changed in the time she'd spent out back—other than her. Without even a glance his way, she went through the doors and into the dining room.

"I'm headed home now," Lucie said as Gabi

approached the front counter—the spiffy, aqua glass-tiled counter that now made her shake her head with bewilderment. "But let me know if you need me."

Gabi smiled. "You were here this morning, and then you came back again a little while ago. What are you, crazy? Go home!"

Lucie shrugged. "You have no idea how many times your family bailed me out since I moved to Lyndon Point and opened my store. I'm glad I can help this time. Just let me know if there's anything else I can do. Otherwise, I'll see you in the morning to help set tables."

"You don't have to."

"I know. I want to. See you then."

As Lucie left, someone tapped Gabi on the shoulder. She turned around, and her jaw gaped wide. "Dee? Is that really you?"

Ryder's younger sister, who'd moved away from Lyndon Point before Gabi graduated from high school, gave her a sheepish smile. "I'm here in the flesh, and I'm back for good this time, not just for my brother's wedding. Well, the plan is to settle back here, as long as they don't run me out of town."

Gabi gave her distant cousin a hug. "I doubt it. The family never stopped talking about you, as though they expected you on the next flight into Sea-Tac."

"That's nice to know." The unexpected touch of insecurity in Dee's eyes caught Gabi by surprise.

"Really, Dee. They must be so happy you're back. I'm surprised no one told me about it."

Dee shrugged. "Big Brother told me you were practically living here and at the animal shelter. I don't know how those two go together, but that would explain why you missed local gossip—" she winked "—er...news."

Gabi noticed Dee's clothes—the black trousers, white shirt, and bow tie. "You're joking, right? You've been waiting tables?"

"I just got here a little while ago. I'm Lucie's replacement." She blew on her nails and rubbed them on her lapel. "And I haven't lost a beat in all these years. Your parents taught me well back in high school."

"We've all put in our time waiting tables here."

"Good thing for you in the middle of a virus outbreak."

"Yes...and no." Gabi shook her head. "Oh, never mind. Thanks, Dee, but I'm back from my break and I can take over your share of tables."

"What, and miss out on all the fun?" Dee winked and sauntered off, her neat black leatherette order notepad and pen in hand. "Let's get together soon and catch up."

How many relatives were going to crawl out of the woodwork? It seemed as though every person who shared even the slightest fraction of DNA with her was determined to put in their time at Tony's. And, contrary to her long-held fears, she hadn't had to field a single disaster the whole day long.

She hadn't been bossed or ordered around, either. Not once.

Relieved, she perched on the stool behind the counter and took a moment to assess the dining room. The tables were full, and no one was waiting to be seated. A glance at the reservations schedule showed her that the next batch of diners would probably show up in the next half hour or so. Before they did, Myra's nieces, who'd come to bus tables, would have their seating ready. Music hummed overhead, and the conversations provided a warm undertone, less animated than at lunch but still lively enough to suggest satisfied customers. The kitchen, as always, had buzzed with lively activity when she'd walked through.

She wondered if the critic was there at the moment.

As soon as the thought crossed her mind, she started to shake. Sympathy bubbled up for Zach, and she felt a strong urge to apologize. She'd hoped to find a moment to approach him as they went about the restaurant's business, but every time she'd come near, he'd turned his attention, as though it was the only thing in the world that mattered.

She'd gotten the message, but she still needed to

speak those words of apology. She needed his forgiveness. Well, in truth, she'd realized she wanted—maybe even needed—more from him, but she was ready to take what he could give. She'd start with his forgiveness and maybe build back up to the warmth they'd shared between them before.

Yes, she was in heart trouble here. And she had no idea what she would do once she left for Cleveland, nor even if he refused her his mercy.

But she had to admit it. She was in love with Zach Davenport. And she didn't have a clue how he felt about her—other than horrified by her actions.

She sighed. She wanted to approach him, to reach out and lay a hand over his, to smooth her fingers down his cheek, to slip into his welcoming arms again. But she didn't dare interrupt his work again, not yet, at any rate. She'd already done enough.

Hours later, when the dining room had emptied and Gabi had tallied up the register totals for the morning's deposit, the only sound in the restaurant came from clanging pans in the kitchen sink and whooshing water in the commercial dishwasher.

"That was fun!" Peter Romano, Aunt Sophia's husband, said as he burst through the swinging kitchen doors.

Behind him, Sam Porter let out a loud laugh. "That's because you spend too many hours sitting around watching TV, now that you've retired. You won't see me closing down my shop before I'm on my way up to heaven."

Gabi hadn't known who Aunt Edna had sent as the cleanup crew until now. "You know you don't have to do this again, right? I have a service that comes every other day, and we take care of things on their off days."

Sam jerked a thumb in Peter's direction. "Maybe you should hire this guy for those off days."

Uncle Peter made a face. "Hey, I can still man a mop. Maybe I should come in and apply for the job."

"Oh, get out of here!" She linked an arm with each of the men. "I appreciate all you've done, but we can take care of things just fine."

Peter placed a soft kiss on her forehead. "I know you can, but we wanted to help. Your parents have done the same when the situation was the other way around. It's what families do."

Gabi locked the door behind the men, her head still reeling after the crazy day. It would take time to sort out all the different emotions she'd experienced since early that morning. She felt as though the earth had shifted beneath her feet, and she no longer knew anything with any certainty.

She did know she had apologies to make. She had decisions to make, too. And she wasn't sure she knew where she should start. The simple prayer she'd shared out back with Zach came to mind.

Maybe a moment with God was the first step on her road back to sanity. She sat in the nearest chair.

She crossed her arms on the table in front of her and laid her forehead down. Peace settled on her as she whispered, "Thank You, Father...thank You."

Long minutes later, footsteps approached. Gabi drew a deep breath. She stood and faced Zach. "I'm sorry—"

"I shouldn't have—"

They laughed, and he waved toward Gabi. "Ladies first."

Great. "Um...I owe you an apology. I sometimes don't listen too well, and barge ahead with my own ideas. It's not the best way to act, and I'm getting too old to keep doing things like that. But it looks like God finally got my attention today." She released a heavy sigh. "I never should have contacted a restaurant critic without talking to you about it first. I would have saved us a lot of stress."

"You're right." At her glare, he gave her a wry chuckle. "But it would have helped if I'd given you a clearer picture of what happened to me in Sacramento. I never wanted to talk about it, never wanted to think about it again. And that's not realistic, either."

"Thanks," she said, relieved they'd made amends. She wouldn't know what she would have done if she'd really created a permanent rift between them. A glimmer of hope burst to life in her heart.

"And thank you."

They stared at each other as the moment lengthened, grew intense, awkward. "Well," she said, "now that we got that straightened out, I'd better go see how many relatives I have to apologize to."

"I don't understand. No one's holding you responsible for a virus."

She shook her head. "It's not the virus I'm worried about. It's the attitude I carried around for a long time that I have to deal with. Oh, and the view of my family that's colored a number of my decisions for longer than it should have."

He crossed his arms. "Go on. This is getting interesting."

"Well, I left here on fire to prove myself far away from my big family—I'm pretty sure I told you that. I did well in school, and then spent years building a career and a life in Cleveland. But when I came back for Papa's sake—and Mama's, too, of course—I brought back with me those same blinders I took with me when I first left. I never once bothered to question anything at all."

A small smile curved his lips. "Then came the virus."

"Then came the virus that brought with it Aunt Edna, Shirley, Aunt Sophia, Lucie, Hannah, Uncle Peter, Myra—do I have to go on?"

He shook his head.

"I left because I'd always felt like a little bleep in

a family that spreads like an amoeba. I felt driven to make something of myself all on my own."

"Would you mind using examples that don't have anything to do with potential infectious organisms?"

Gabi laughed until her eyes teared up. "No amoeba images necessary. I was so afraid I would always be viewed as nothing more than a shadow within my huge family, always dependent on them, that I basically ran away. But can you imagine what would have happened to me if I'd had to handle something like today in Cleveland? I would have been on my own there."

"From personal experience, I can assure you that when disaster strikes—real disaster, not a couple of sick employees—what you really want nearby is that big comforting family that can come around you like a hug. Remember? It happened to me after my parents died."

She winced, shook her head at her foolishness. "In spite of how hard I fought it, when I look back now, it feels pretty good to know how much they care. They all set aside their work to come and help."

"Would you have helped them if they'd needed you?"

How could he ask? "But, of course!"

He only smiled.

She blushed. "You made your point. I am starting to figure it out."

"There's something else you've managed to miss.

God didn't make you to vanish into the shadow of your family. You can trust Him to guide you next time you're afraid they'll swallow you up or they might overrun your choices."

"Yes, but I thought I knew where God was leading me, and I messed up."

"I recognized the gifts God gave me, developed those gifts and opened my restaurant. The salmonella infection ruined my restaurant. And while I know God didn't send the salmonella, I can see how He's working good out of that mess. He brought me here to Lyndon Point, didn't He?"

"But you lost your job at the shelter, too."

He smiled reflectively. "From the way things look right now, things may be working out in a way that will bring God more glory in the end. The restaurant's still standing, doing business, making money, right?"

She nodded.

"And there's my shelter."

"I'll withhold judgment until I see what kind of glory that wreck on the outskirts of town will bring. Or did that deal fall apart?"

He grinned. "On the contrary. Edna called late this afternoon. Your news about the critic pushed my news out of my head. My financing went through. Myra's son will do the renovations, and we plan to open the shelter right after New Year's."

A burst of joy filled her. "I'm so happy for you. I

know how much this means to you. You're so good with the animals, and you ran the shelter so well. I admire what you did there, and know where your heart is." But then, dismay struck and she teetered between the two warring emotions. "Oh, no. Is that when Antonio's loses its marvelous new chef?"

He grew serious. "I don't know. Helping you has shown me again how much I love to run a kitchen. Maybe there's a middle road for me."

Hope flickered. "Maybe you and I can negotiate terms with Papa so that you can...oh, I don't know, stay on as head chef while Claudia manages your private shelter?"

"Throw in a percentage ownership, and then you're talking."

"Papa's a pretty shrewd businessman. He might just take you up on that. Especially if you throw in the pizzas, spaghetti and meatballs, lasagna and his trademark garlic bread for the lunch crowd."

"When he's better, we'll talk." Then Zach grew serious. "What about you?"

"I'm not sure about me. I didn't want to come home, but I did. I wanted to go back to Cleveland, but I couldn't. Now, I might have reached the point where I can—and have to—go back, but I'm not sure what I want to do."

"That's about as clear as a layer of mozzarella on a Tony's Garbage Pie."

"And just about that sticky."

"Could I add another layer to your choice?"

"Will it make the other layers disappear?"

His eyes began to twinkle again. "I don't think *disappear* is the right word. It might make them easier to cut through. But that's for you to decide."

"Hmm… That doesn't sound like you're going to help."

"Look, if there's one thing I've learned," he told her, "it's that I can always lean on God. He's always trustworthy, and He can always work things out to my benefit." He released a jagged breath. "What I'm trying to say is that you should trust that God planted you in the middle of the perfect family for you. Go ahead and trust the love and support that big, warm, loving family of yours has for you—it's not a control thing."

"I think I'm on the way there."

"It might help when you recognize that God, in His grace, will always bring you back to the exact place He made for you in *His* eternal family."

"He's going to have to show me a lot about this planting business, because I'm lost when it comes to what I'm going to do next—where He's planting me these days."

"Trust Him," Zach said, taking her hands in his. "And here comes the part that might just make your decision stickier for you. Trust me, too. I'll never lose track of who you are. You're unique, and you've come to mean too much to me. I promise you I'll always treasure this relationship that's begun to grow between us, even though I don't think either one of us can be sure where it's going to wind up. I know where I want it to, though!" He grew serious again. "Please tell me you recognize what's grown between us, too."

She blushed, stunned by his intensity. Was this real? Could it be happening? To her? "I know it's there, and those feelings are going to make some of my decisions harder to make."

"Maybe I can help with those decisions. Make them easier instead."

Gabi caught her breath as the love in her heart burst into sparks of happiness, soared into her head, swirled and left her giddy at the possibilities. Could her dreams really be coming true?

Still, she had to make sure. "I don't see how throwing you into the mix could—"

"Oh, no. We're not throwing me into the mix. My plan is to sway you toward choosing in my favor."

Joy and thankfulness welled up inside her, and she could barely get the words out. "How are you going to do that?" she whispered.

"Like this." And then he kissed her.

Again and again.

Epilogue

"Are you ready to cut the ribbon?" Zach asked Gabi.

"I have the giant scissors right here." She waved the garden clipping shears he'd given her.

"Well, then, let's go."

They walked out hand in hand to meet the gathered residents of Lyndon Point. It was unseasonably warm for January, and Gabi wondered if they'd have enough refreshments for the growing crowd. They'd advertised the opening of Zach's new private shelter in local papers, a small ad in the front window at Antonio's, and in every other business in town.

The animals had stayed in their old location after Zach had come to an agreement with the town council. They kept his salary in exchange for rent until the cats and dogs could be moved. Once again, Gabi's large family had stepped up, and the move had taken place three days before.

Houdini had come along every step of the way, at Papa's side, proud in his brand-new red jacket. He'd gone legit, no more a jailbird, but rather her father's therapy dog.

Now, the shelter was ready to screen adoptive families, to receive new rescues and to offer the town the same services the old location had.

Gabi had moved back to Lyndon Point, but instead of listening to Edna and looking for a job in Seattle, she'd taken over managing Antonio's. Zach kept the executive chef position, and everyone agreed they made the perfect team for the restaurant's future.

A bright and rosy one, especially after the restaurant critic had written high praise for Zach's cooking and for the excellent service she'd received. In the months since that first time, she'd come, introduced herself to Zach and Gabi and had even brought guests with her on her third visit.

Even Papa thought the restaurant was headed in the right direction, especially now that he'd recovered enough to go back to work on a part-time basis. He preferred the lunch crowd, as did his wife. Neither of the older Carlinis could contain their pride when they boasted about their daughter, the restaurant's manager. They especially touted its family ownership with family appeal—but with a gourmet twist.

And today, it was poised to become even more of

a family affair. The day before, Antonio and Zach had signed the legal paperwork to make Zach minority partner in the restaurant. Gabi couldn't wait to make the announcement to the residents of Lyndon Point after they cut the ribbon they'd stretched across the new shelter's front door. They had so much to celebrate.

Ryder met them at the center of the ribbon's expanse. "Are you guys ready?"

Houdini barked his response.

Everyone laughed.

Zach reached down and scratched the little matchmaker's head. "I've been ready for the longest time."

The mayor nodded toward the high school marching band's drum line, who then set up a thunderous drumroll. With all due ceremony, Gabi and Zach clasped their hands over the handles of the shears, and the ribbon dropped into two swathes.

"But wait," she cried, after the clapping had gone on for a couple of minutes. "There's more. As the manager of Antonio's, I'd like to announce a new era for the restaurant."

"Aw, come on, Gabi," Uncle Peter yelled. "Aren't you busy enough yet? What new crazy plan have you come up with now?"

"You'll like this one!" She turned to the man at her side. "Papa and Zach have signed the contracts, and Antonio's is a brand-new partnership."

More applause. This time, however, Zach raised

a hand to silence it. "And there's even more. I'd like to invite you to another launch. That one won't happen until next June, but Gabi and I would like to have every one there, too."

"What's that all about?" Aunt Edna asked.

Zach took Gabi's hand, turned it to the crowd and showed off her ring finger. "It's all about this, and all about us. Gabi's finally home to stay. She's agreed to stay forever at my side as my wonderful wife! Join us for our wedding as we launch our new family."

No one silenced the applause that time. Zach was too busy kissing his future bride.

* * * * *

Dear Reader,

The Pacific Northwest has a well-deserved reputation for rugged beauty and spectacular views. I agree, but I'm biased, since my family lives in a waterfront town just outside Seattle, very much like Lyndon Point. But as beautiful as that part of the county is, it's not the panorama that tugs at my heart and draws me there. It is, of course, those I love.

A Daughter's Homecoming is about a family, a hometown and a dog who needs a loving home—a dog who brings together two people who've been running away from their pasts. A daughter returns to town when her parents need her the most; a man moves to town in search of a place to call home. As they work together, they learn to trust God and let Him heal their wounds. He blesses them with perspective for the past, purpose for the present and hope for the future.

I hope you enjoy reading Gabi and Zach's story as much I enjoyed writing about things I love: Puget Sound, great food and a scrappy rescue dog—very much like my two rescued terriers.

My prayer for you, my readers, is that my story leaves you with a warm heart, a happy laugh and the hope of your faith.

You can always contact me on Facebook, by email at ginnyaiken@gmail.com or on my webpage at www.ginnyaiken.com. Of course, mail will reach me through my publisher, too. I love to hear from readers!

Blessings,

Questions for Discussion

1. Gabi carried a burden of hurts from her childhood into adulthood. What kind of events or experiences in your past do you still keep alive in your memory?

2. Gabi left Washington State to run away from her past, but because her family remains in Lyndon Point, she can't really escape it. Has there been a time in your life when you tried to deal with an issue by running from it? How did it turn out? What would you do differently?

3. Zach did the same thing as Gabi when he suffered a business failure—the only difference was that his escape was as an adult. What Scripture verses might help one cope after a major failure without the need to flee?

4. Sometimes blessings come in the oddest of packages—Houdini is a good example of this. How would you have responded in Gabi's place?

5. Most people take in a "stray" of one kind or another at least once in their life. What kind of impact did your "stray" have on you?

6. Zach was able to pull up roots, since he had nothing left to keep him in Sacramento. He was

seeking a fresh start in Lyndon Point, where he was welcomed. That isn't always the case. Have you moved to begin a new phase of your life? If so, what was your experience?

7. What would it take for you to take a step as drastic as the one Zach took?

8. Gabi kept her contact with the restaurant critic secret with the best of intentions—to surprise Zach. Have you faced unintended consequences when you've tried to do something you thought would be nice for someone else? What would have produced a better outcome?

9. What do you think was the root cause of Gabi's desire to surprise Zach?

10. Trust becomes an issue for Zach as a result of Gabi contacting the critic. What drew them back together and restored their relationship? Have you gone through a similar situation?

11. How would you counsel a friend who is going through something similar to what Gabi and Zach went through?

12. Although Gabi harbored a somewhat off-kilter view of her family, including her parents, when Papa became ill, she flew right back home to

help. How has the commandment to "honor your parents" played out in your life, when you were the child and/or the parent?

13. A person can sometimes become spiritually blind to where it takes desperation to surrender their image of themselves and their capabilities. Can you relate to Gabi's eye-opening moment, when she gains a new understanding of her family and their intentions? When in your past have you gone through an experience like hers?

14. The Pacific Northwest is undoubtedly magnificent in its beauty, and Lyndon Point, regardless of her memories, exerts a tug on Gabi's heart. Is there a place where your heart longs to return? What caused you to leave? What keeps you away?

LARGER-PRINT BOOKS!

GET 2 FREE
LARGER-PRINT NOVELS
PLUS 2 FREE
MYSTERY GIFTS

Love Inspired

Larger-print novels are now available...

YES! Please send me 2 FREE LARGER-PRINT Love Inspired® novels and my 2 FREE mystery gifts (gifts are worth about $10). After receiving them, if I don't wish to receive any more books, I can return the shipping statement marked "cancel." If I don't cancel, I will receive 6 brand-new novels every month and be billed just $5.24 per book in the U.S. or $5.74 per book in Canada. That's a savings of at least 23% off the cover price. It's quite a bargain! Shipping and handling is just 50¢ per book in the U.S. and 75¢ per book in Canada.* I understand that accepting the 2 free books and gifts places me under no obligation to buy anything. I can always return a shipment and cancel at any time. Even if I never buy another book, the two free books and gifts are mine to keep forever.

122/322 IDN F49Y

Name _____ (PLEASE PRINT)

Address _____ Apt. # _____

City _____ State/Prov. _____ Zip/Postal Code _____

Signature (if under 18, a parent or guardian must sign) _____

Mail to the Harlequin® Reader Service:
IN U.S.A.: P.O. Box 1867, Buffalo, NY 14240-1867
IN CANADA: P.O. Box 609, Fort Erie, Ontario L2A 5X3

**Are you a current subscriber to Love Inspired books
and want to receive the larger-print edition?
Call 1-800-873-8635 or visit www.ReaderService.com.**

* Terms and prices subject to change without notice. Prices do not include applicable taxes. Sales tax applicable in N.Y. Canadian residents will be charged applicable taxes. Offer not valid in Quebec. This offer is limited to one order per household. Not valid for current subscribers to Love Inspired Larger-Print books. All orders subject to credit approval. Credit or debit balances in a customer's account(s) may be offset by any other outstanding balance owed by or to the customer. Please allow 4 to 6 weeks for delivery. Offer available while quantities last.

Your Privacy—The Harlequin® Reader Service is committed to protecting your privacy. Our Privacy Policy is available online at www.ReaderService.com or upon request from the Harlequin Reader Service.

We make a portion of our mailing list available to reputable third parties that offer products we believe may interest you. If you prefer that we not exchange your name with third parties, or if you wish to clarify or modify your communication preferences, please visit us at www.ReaderService.com/consumerchoice or write to us at Harlequin Reader Service Preference Service, P.O. Box 9062, Buffalo, NY 14269. Include your complete name and address.

LILPDIR13R